SEVEN WOMEN

SEVEN WOMEN

MICHAEL HEMMINGSON

BORGO PRESS

For Sage Tune—fan of a good detective story

SEVEN WOMEN

Published by Borgo Press.
www.wildsidebooks.com

In a marriage, you had to lie, it was all a tissue of lies like a play…but living alone necessitated telling the truth.

—Joyce Carol Oates

CHAPTER 1 . . .

I've been sitting at the counter of this bar for almost an hour, now on my third drink, when I notice one of the women, in a group of women, saunter in and sit in a booth. There are five of them, all in their mid-twenties to early thirties. I don't want to seem too conspicuous. I try to verify my suspicion from the mirror at the bar. There are too many bottles in the way. I turn around and look. Yes, it's her—my ex-wife. She sees me looking, no expression on her face, quickly goes back to her four friends—smiling and laughing, as if I don't exist.

The best thing to do—get up and leave, go home or to another bar. I thought this would be an uncomplicated day—come in and have a few drinks, go home and maybe watch some television. Now she enters the narrative, much in the same way she originally came in: without preamble.

I haven't seen my ex-wife in five months. She wears a gray blazer, white blouse, dark skirt. She's just off work, I assume; she's an associate editor at a mass-market paperback publisher. Her friends don't look as if they're in publishing; they don't have that fatigued demeanor many of her colleagues have. I wonder who they are.

I get another drink. I hear them laughing and talking, and I feel small. I can see her face in the mirror now: long black hair, fair skin. I remember things. I hate it when you drink and remember. Drinking alone isn't a good thing sometimes. These women have the right idea: come in as a group. You get less melancholy. I don't have any drinking buddies.

I get up and go to the bathroom. I feel her looking at me, although she'd never admit it. One of her friends, a blonde, glances my way; she whispers something to the woman next to her. Short dark hair. I don't believe I know any of them. I never knew her friends that well. We had an isolated-from-the-world kind of marriage—eight months in all.

In the men's room, I decide I'm going to do it. What the hell. It would be uncivilized, after all, not to say hello.

I go to the bar first, freshen my drink, and make my way over to the booth and the five women. My ex-wife is at one end, the blonde who looked at me at the other. My ex-wife sees me coming and flips the hair out of her eyes, trying to ignore me. The other women look my way; one giggles. They're expectant. Maybe they think I have a line, that I want to come on to them all. How the hell do I know what women think?

"Hello, Tasha."

My ex-wife looks up. "Hi."

"Tasha," one of the women—a redhead—says, "Is this someone we should know about?"

"This is Leonard, my ex-husband," she tells them.

"Oh," one of them says, "the mysterious ex-hubby."

I feel sweaty all of the sudden.

"Hello," they say to me.

"Hello," I say back.

"Hey," says the blonde, "why don't you join us?"

Tasha starts to say something, but two others say, "Hey, that'd be fun. We should have a guy here, get his impressions."

"I'm sure Leonard has things to do," my ex-wife says.

"I was just sitting over there drinking," I say. "Just wanted to say—hello."

"We're drinking, too," the blonde says. "That's what you do in a bar. Drink and talk and bullshit. Why don't you join us? There's plenty of room, and I don't think Tasha would really mind—would you, Tasha?"

My ex-wife brushes the hair from her eyes again, glares at me as the hair falls back. "No, I wouldn't mind. What the hell."

Yeah, what the hell. Our favorite phrase from a failed union. Tasha moves into the booth, next to the redhead. The blonde nods. I sit next to my ex-wife and feel fucked. She's trying to prove something to them, to me, maybe to herself, I don't know. That she can keep calm and cool in my presence? That the marriage is behind her now? Or does she want to show her friends what an asshole I was, a memento mori of her past?

I'm a little drunk and a little lonely and I don't care, so I sit next to my ex-wife and look at these women and wait for anything.

CHAPTER 2 . . .

"We're kind of like a club," the blonde says.

"We're not a club," the redhead says.

Tasha is observing me with one eye. I want to ask her how she's been. They're all drinking wine, except for the blonde, who's having a beer.

The blonde, I find out, is Amelia; she's an elementary school teacher. The redhead is Sheila, a hostess in a restaurant uptown. The woman with short dark hair is Cara, a jazz musician; and the last woman, rather quiet, Lisa, who has brown hair—she's a writer.

I smile. "You all have names that end with 'A'."

"Except Holly," Amelia says. "Holly isn't here yet."

"Holly's always late," Sheila says.

"That's the charm of Holly," Cara says. "Fashionably late."

"She's a nerd," Amelia says to me. "She's into computers."

"Nerd doesn't fit," Lisa finally talks. "She dresses better than a nerd. But she is very smart," she adds, looking at me. "She programs things."

"Computers," Amelia says, taking a long pull from her beer bottle.

"So," Sheila says to me, "what do you do, Leonard?" She seems tipsy.

"Well," I say.

"He works at a private investigation agency," Tasha says as if she were tasting something bad. Maybe it's the wine. "Or at least he used to. Do you still work at Grape and Manor, Len?"

I drink my drink. "Yeah."

"A private eye?" Lisa says, sitting up.

"Something like that," I say.

"Didn't you write a private-eye novel?" Sheila asks Lisa.

"I tried writing one," Lisa says, shrugging. "They're popular, and I was going to have a woman dick, because that's real in right now, but the book didn't work. That's not the kind of stuff I write."

"What do you write?" I ask.

"Books," she says.

"Is that how you know Tasha?"

"Yes," Tasha answers for her.

"You don't look like a private eyeball," Amelia tells me. "Aren't you supposed to have one of those hats—a fedora? And a trench coat or something? Aren't you supposed to talk like that one guy—the guy in the old black-and-white movies, you know?"

"Actually, dear, I do own a fedora and a long trench," I say in my best Bogart impersonation, "When I'm out chasing the bad guys."

"Oh!" Amelia kicks me with her leg. "That gives me goose bumps!"

"Huh," from my ex-wife, shaking her head.

"Everything gives you goose bumps," Sheila says, and then adds, to me: "We were thinking of nicknaming her 'Goose bump.'"

"The only nickname I have is 'Amnesia,'" Amelia says.

Lisa leans forward. "You never told us the story behind that nickname."

"I know."

"Maybe she will tonight," Cara says.

Amelia sips her beer, sees that it's empty, and says, "Maybe I will." She waves for the waitress.

"So do you really go after bad guys?" Sheila asks me. "Do you follow people around? Do you carry a gun? Do you peep on husbands cheating on their wives?"

"Or even vice versa," Lisa says.

"No," Tasha says, "he doesn't do those things."

"I don't usually carry a gun," I say. "It's not necessary. Most of my work involves doing background checks on people applying for certain jobs, and serving court papers on people."

Amelia asks, "You don't sit in your office and wait for sexy women in wide-brimmed hats and skirts with high slits wanting you to solve mysteries?"

"It's never like that," I say. "It's usually boring."

"It is," Tasha says.

The waitress comes to the table. I insist on buying the round. Amelia orders a beer and the others all want wine, white, except for Lisa, who has red. I ask for a refill of my vodka tonic.

"So," I say, "you ladies get together once a week and shoot the bull?"

"Lady?" Sheila says mockingly. "Who are you calling a lady?"

"Sorry. Women. Girls?" I grin.

Sheila says, "I still like being called a girl. In three months I'm going to be thirty fucking years old."

The waitress returns with new drinks and I give her a twenty, tell her to keep the change. I sip my drink.

"One day I want to write a book, any kind of book." Amelia shrugs. "I don't know what it'll be about."

"Let's not talk about books," Tasha says. "I've been talking books all day. I'm sick of books."

Silence as we drink.

"We can talk about men," Cara says.

"We always talk about men," Sheila says.

Amelia says, "Men are an endless topic."

"Endless is the word," Sheila says.

My ex-wife gives me another quick look.

"Do we need men?" Lisa says.

I'm enjoying this.

"You don't if you're a lesbian," Amelia says.

I want to touch Tasha at this moment. I am remembering Veronica, a friend of hers. One night, during our marriage, we took her to bed, and afterwards, things were never the same. I watched Tasha get caught up in the swarm of that evening, the alcohol and the drugs and the sex we couldn't control. Then I believed that evening was a watershed, that it marked the decline of our marriage. And yes, it did.

Tasha says, "We need men."

"I need men," Amelia says, looking at me from her beer, "but that's because I like men. All sorts of men, as long as they're not fat or sweaty or dumb."

"Ah," I say.

"So, Leonard," Sheila says to me. "When you get together with your buddies, your guy pals, what do you fellas talk about the most? You probably talk about women."

I really don't have any buddies, not the kind I get together with. I'm pretty much a loner, and always have been. Tasha knows this.

"Sometimes what we talk about is we talk about women," I say.

"Or sports," Cara says.

"I'm really not into sports."

"I like sports," Amelia says. "I like football. I like to watch football on TV."

"You just like to look at the players," Cara says.

"All those cute butts," Amelia says. "Oh, yes."

"I went out with a football player in high school," Lisa says.

"Really?"

"A dumb jock. I didn't go out with him for long. I don't know why I dated him in the first place. He was cute, sure, and a lot of the girls at school wanted him, but he didn't have crap up here," she adds, pointing to her temple.

"Stereotype," Tasha says, "I'm sure not all football players are dumb jocks."

"I agree," Lisa says, "but this fellow happened to be one."

"So did you sleep with him?" Sheila wants to know.

"No."

"No?"

"We only went out for a short time."

"But I bet he tried to get some," Cara says into her wine.

"He tried, and failed."

"I never slept with a football player," Amelia says. "I think it'd be interesting."

"You would," Sheila smiles.

"Look how I'm talking," Amelia says, "I wonder what Leonard here is thinking."

"He thinks you're a horn-dog," Cara says.

"I'm just being honest."

"Call her a horn-dog," Cara tells me.

"If you feel uncomfortable talking with me here—" I say to Amelia.

"Not me," Amelia answers. "I'm always honest."

"We don't want Leonard to leave," Sheila says.

Tasha looks at me. "How's Jay?"

"He's okay."

"Who's Jay?" Sheila asks.

"A good friend of mine," I say. "He paints. His work is in the galleries now and then." I add, "He's a friend of Tasha's, too."

"I went out with a painter once," Cara says. "He always smelled like paint. That really bugged me."

"What did he paint?" Lisa asks.

"Houses."

"I think Leonard is talking about a real artist," Amelia says.

"Artist, yes," Tasha says, touching her wine glass.

"Is he an artist," Cara asks, "or a 'real' artist?"

"Is there a difference?" Sheila says.

Lisa answers, "Yes."

Tasha says, "All that's academic. Philosophical."

"Philosophy is horse manure," Sheila says.

"Or house manure, if you're a painter," Amelia says.

"Touché," I say.

"All those philosophers did was sit in French cafés and bullshit."

"Kind of like what we're doing now," Cara says.

"I've never been to France," Sheila says.

"I've never been anywhere," Amelia says, "except to outer space."

Lisa smiles. "I was in France one summer. I was nineteen, going all over Europe. It was an experience."

"Yeah," Cara says.

"I really went into outer space, in a UFO," Amelia says quietly at the same time Tasha says, "Leonard is French."

There's a brief pause when we all try to decide whether or not Amelia actually said that. Then she says, "Oh, you're French?"

"Half French," I say.

"Which half?" Sheila asks.

I say, "My mother is French, my father is American."

"You have dual citizenship?" Lisa says.

"No. I'm all American."

"You don't have an accent," Amelia says.

"I was there when I was really young," I say.

"Then he came here," Tasha says.

"Have you ever gone back?" Lisa asks.

"I used to," I say.

Tasha says, "I wonder where Holly is?"

"Late," Lisa says.

"As always," Sheila says.

"Subways and buses," Amelia says. "I used to drive when I lived upstate. I would drive toward the mountains and look at them. Sometimes I'd think I could drive forever, on and on, going anywhere and everywhere, leaving my past behind."

"I hate cars," Tasha says. "They have no respect for space."

"Or pavement," Lisa adds.

"Are our feet competing with cars?" Amelia says. She seems confused, drinks her beer. I wonder what is really on her mind. I shouldn't speak. I should just listen. I have always been a good listener. I make a fool out of myself when

I talk and drink. Talking and drinking don't always mix well.

"So," Sheila says.

"So," Amelia says.

"So," Cara says.

"I have to go to the bathroom," Tasha says.

I get up so she can get out. I sit back in the booth, and I'm next to Sheila now. I see that her skirt is hiked up some from her position, charcoal gray nylons. I find her attractive. I find them all attractive.

Amelia kicks me with her foot. "Oh, sorry," she says.

"So," Sheila says to me.

"So," I say.

"You must feel a little weird."

"Yeah?"

"Tasha," she says.

"Well."

"That's not what I mean," Sheila says.

"It's okay," I say.

"She hasn't said a lot about you," Sheila says.

"Well," I say.

Cara says, "You're putting him on the spot. Poor Leonard."

"Am I making you feel uncomfortable?" Sheila asks, leaning close, her hand brushing my leg.

"Not at all," I smile, and it's no lie.

I do feel weird.

"Where did you and Tasha meet?" Amelia asks.

"It's a strange story."

"I like strange stories."

"No talking about Tasha while she's gone," Lisa says. "That's not nice."

"Sorry," Amelia says.

"Now I bet you feel like you're on the spot," Sheila says.

"Me?" I say. "Never."

She has red lipstick, thick lips. I like her mouth. I like her hair.

"You're a private eye?" Cara asks me.

"That's me."

"My brother is a cop," Cara says, "and his wife is always worried about him. Afraid he'll get shot. She's a nervous wreck. I could never be married to a cop."

"I could never be married to a nervous wreck," Amelia says.

"I don't think I could ever be married," Lisa says.

"Why not?" Amelia asks.

"I want to get married one day," Lisa explains. "I've never really met anyone I wanted to marry . . . or who wanted to marry me. My mother keeps bothering me about it. 'Lisa, why aren't you married?' She wants grandchildren."

"I can't see myself as anyone's grandmother," Sheila says.

"It'll happen one day," Cara tells her. "It happens to everyone."

"First I need to have a kid of my own," Sheila says, shaking her head. "And the thought of having a kid is so alien to me. But I guess this is something I should really be thinking about since I'm almost thirty. Oh, Jesus, this is depressing, let's talk about something else, please."

"I—" Amelia starts.

We look at her.

She shrugs and drinks her beer.

Tasha returns. I start to get up, but she sits down, wedging me between herself and Sheila.

"Did I miss anything?" she asks.

"We were talking about kids," Cara says, "or the idea of having them. And then about having grandchildren."

I feel something coming from Tasha, but she only says, "Oh."

"Actually," Sheila says, "we were grilling Leonard for info on where you and he met oh-so-long-ago, if it was that oh-so-long-ago."

"Well," my ex-wife says, "it's a weird story."

CHAPTER 3 . . .

Amelia says, "I like weird stories."

"We shouldn't talk about me," I say.

"I was engaged once," Cara says, "believe it or not."

"You never mentioned that before," Sheila says.

"I know. It wasn't worth mentioning."

"What happened?" Amelia asks.

"I was eighteen. Maybe it is worth mentioning, now that I think about it. I was in love."

"A first love?" asks Lisa.

"I guess you could call it that," Cara says.

"If you were engaged to the guy, I'd say you were in love with him," Sheila says.

"That's a good point," Cara says. "I met him in my senior year of high school. The romance didn't really begin until after graduation, during summer. It was a strange time because no one really knew what they were going to do. Some of us had enrolled in junior colleges; others were going to state universities or off to school elsewhere. Some of us did nothing, partied through the summer. Maybe it was a hard concept, that high school was over, and real life was beginning. I had my bass guitar, you know, and I was still looking for the right band. I did my blues and jazz jams at these places every weekend. Guys thought I was strange. I played the bass, I was a girl, they didn't know how to react to me.

"Stephen—the guy I got engaged to—was a saxophone player. He was all right, not that great, not as great as he dreamt to be, because he had something missing. I don't know what. That 'something' a musician needs to have to rise above the rest. Anyway, we were going out. It started off as, well, there's this guy I like, I enjoy hanging out with him, playing some music, and I like having sex with him, he's not that bad a lover, at least I can talk to him, right? He got serious first. I heard 'I love you' from his lips and this was long after we started having sex. I didn't know how to take it. I didn't love him. I guess I did later. It's the sort of thing that grows on you. I cared for him. So—next thing you know we're talking marriage.

"Maybe it was his parents who got him into that; we were spending so much time together and neither of us knew what we were going to do so maybe his parents said, 'Marry the girl and get a job and start a family,' because that's what they did, right? But we weren't formally engaged—I didn't get a diamond ring. He couldn't afford it. We could barely afford anything, we were poor musicians to the T, scraping up dimes and pennies to do anything, like buying gas for his car. I didn't care about a ring. He said, 'Why don't we get married?' and I said, 'Sure.' It seemed like the thing to do, and the sex was better, and I really liked being with him, and so I figured if it stayed that way for the rest of my life, I could be content. We were 'engaged' for a year or so. I don't know, maybe we would've never married, but I started to like the idea of having a fiancé. It worked well when guys would hit on me and I had no interest. I could just say, 'Hey, look, I'm engaged to be married.' None of them ever asked, 'Where's your ring, then?'

"I don't know when it started to fall apart. Maybe we were too used to each other. Maybe the love wasn't really there. I was working this job at a fast food place. You know the kind of job, they suck. I needed money. I couldn't stand it. I burned one of my playing fingers on hot grease, and I said, Screw this, I'm not going to risk losing my playing fingers over minimum wage, so I quit.

"I took the bus to Stephen's house. He wasn't working, just sitting around his parents' house playing his saxophone. I go into the backyard, go to his window. I expect to hear him playing. I do hear music, and it's rock. I thought, 'That's funny.' I look into his window and see him screwing Anna Loren, this girl from school, one of the what you'd call 'sluts.' He's right there humping away and she's crying out Oh Steve oh Steve and all that. I just went, 'Wow.'"

"So what did you do?" Sheila asks. "Did you pound on the window?"

"No. I walked home. It was a long walk, but I needed it."

"Wow," says Amelia.

"I would've picked up a rock and thrown it through his window," Lisa says.

"I thought of that," Cara says. "But what would have been the point? It was—it was the end of something. It was over. In a way, I was relieved. I guess I never had any intention of marrying him after all. So I went home. I called him on the phone."

Tasha says, "You told him off."

"No. I called him later. I told him I quit my job. 'Why?' he asked. I told him why. 'Oh,' he said, and asked if I wanted him to come pick me up and maybe we could go somewhere. 'How's Anna?' I said and told him I bet she loved that rock group, the one that was playing while they were doing it. He was real quiet for a moment, probably trying to figure it out. Then he said, 'Cara, I'm sorry, I don't know what to say.' 'Don't say anything,' I told him and that was it. No argument, no nothing. It was like an understanding between us. It was over. It was never meant to be."

"I caught a boyfriend cheating on me when I was around the same age as you were," Sheila says. "I caught him with one of my friends. But the break-up wasn't as smooth as that, no way. There were a lot of words. I wanted to scratch his fucking eyes out. But what I did—I wanted to get him back—I went out and fucked his best friend. I just went to this guy's house pretending to look like I was looking for my boyfriend. I was dressed to kill in denim shorts and a halter; I was a number back then. Jesus, we're talking like a decade ago. So I seduce his best friend. He was game. It was pretty fun, but then I felt bad. You know—I don't know.

"The problem was, I couldn't get rid of this guy for weeks. We have sex once and suddenly he thinks I'm his. He kept calling. I had to change my number. He started coming to my door. I told him I would call the cops if he didn't go away. 'You're a whore,' he said to me, 'you're a real whore.' Problem was, I kind of felt like one. No. I felt bad. I didn't know how to tell him I was using him to get back at the boyfriend. How could I? I mean, how do you explain that to a guy without looking like—something bad? A whore, something like that. It took me a while to feel better about myself."

"We all do rash things now and then," Tasha says.

"Yes, we do," I say, looking at my ex-wife.

Amelia finishes her beer. "I'm out of beer." She waves at the waitress again.

CHAPTER 4 . . .

"It's a sad thing," Amelia says, "when you're out of beer."

"I'll have a vodka tonic this time," Tasha tells the waitress.

"Same here," I say.

"Well," Cara says, "I'll have a tequila sunrise."

"Another," Amelia holds up her beer.

Lisa sticks to wine.

I look at Sheila and imagine myself the old boyfriend's best friend she seduced. I picture her ten years younger, in shorts and a halter, coming to my door. I see myself taking her into the bedroom, stripping her clothes off, knowing she's my best friend's girl but not caring because I want to stick myself inside her.

"It was difficult at first, running into Stephen now and then," Cara says. "Our city was small. A town. We didn't talk. Then we started to talk. We were still friends. At least we were still friends."

"Was he still with the slut?" Amelia asks.

"No. She changed guys every week or two."

"She's probably dead now," Sheila says.

"Funny you should say that because the last I heard—about a year ago—she went to the West Coast and was modeling in cheap porn videos and walking the streets in L.A. But that could have been a rumor. You know how rumors are, especially in a small city."

"I could really start ranting about the porn industry," Lisa says, "and what it does to some women. But I won't."

Amelia giggles. "I once let a guy take nudie pictures of me."

"I bet you did," Sheila says.

"I thought it was kinda neat. I was fifteen."

"Fifteen?" I say.

"How old was he?" Tasha asks.

"I'm not sure," Amelia says, "maybe twenty-eight or so."

"That's illegal," Lisa says. "It may be even kiddie porn, if you were fifteen. He could have gone to jail."

"Jail?" Amelia says. "Maybe, if I told. But I wasn't going to tell. I liked him."

"Did you sleep with him?" Cara asks.

"No. I just let him take nudie pictures of me. It was innocent, really."

The waitress returns with our drinks.

"Okay," Amelia reaches into her jeans pocket, "I'll get this one."

CHAPTER 5 . . .

"At least I have money," she adds, pulling wadded bills from her pocket, along with several paper clips, two stamps, and someone's business card.

Cara reaches for the business card. "A temp agency?"

"Yeah," Amelia answers.

"But you have a job."

"Who knows for how long, with all the cutbacks in the schools. I'm not even making very much as it is. I was thinking of moonlighting, filing, or word-processing, bring in some extra money, or maybe finding a full-time job through temping, one that pays better than a teacher's salary. And if I get laid off, I'm going to need to find a job really fast."

"Let's not talk about jobs and money," Sheila says. "That shit depresses me."

"Tell me about it," Amelia says, and smiles. "There was a problem with the payroll checks once. They were over a week late. I was really stressed. My rent was due, I barely had any food, and I didn't have a dime. I was ready to walk the streets and make a quick fifty."

"You don't mean that," Lisa says.

"I don't, but think about it. How far would any of us go if it came down to immediate survival?" She straightens out the bills on the table. "All for this green paper. I hate this green paper."

"Really, let's not talk about money," Sheila says.

Tasha nods. "Let's not."

"Sorry," says Amelia.

Sheila says, "Not that I'm hurting right now, thank the

lucky stars, but there were times I was really destitute and I'd rather not remember those times."

I know that feeling. I sip my drink.

"Anyway," Tasha raises her voice.

"Anyway," Sheila says. "Enough of that."

Silence as we drink.

"So," Cara says to Lisa, "how's the new book coming along?"

"Sluggishly," Lisa says, "but I'm getting there."

"What's it about?" I ask.

"Sex, death, sex, and love," Sheila says, "isn't that what any good book is about?"

"Isn't that what everything's about?" Cara says. "Movies, plays, music—you name it?"

Lisa says, "They're categorizing it as 'romantic suspense.' They'll sell it in grocery-store stands and chains. Just like my last one."

"Actually, it's rather good," Tasha says. "It's genre, but quality genre. Lisa fleshes out her characters nicely; you really get to know them. That's the charm of her work."

Sheila laughs, touching my ex-wife's arm. "You're supposed to say that, hon. You're her editor."

"I wouldn't say it if I didn't mean it," Tasha answers. "I have to edit some real crap sometimes. And I do mean crap, the romances and mysteries, but they bring in the bucks, so who cares if they're crap?"

"You accept crap?" from Amelia.

"They're not my acquisitions. As an associate editor, I sometimes get dumped with excess workload from the senior editors, or if an editor leaves and the orphaned books are disseminated around the office, I have to take one."

"I think that would be a cool job," Amelia says. "Sitting around the office all day reading books."

Tasha laughs. "I hardly ever read anything at the office. I'm on the phone, in meetings, checking galleys, talking with the marketing crew. I do all my reading at home. Nights, weekends. Hell, I'm always on the job. It seems like the only time I ever really get out is these weekly Thursday night get-togethers."

"Maybe you need a man in your life," Cara says.

Awkward silence. Tasha sips her drink. Cara looks at me, flushes.

"Don't we all," Sheila says.

"Except Leonard," Amelia says.

"Except Leonard, of course."

"You have a man," Cara says to Sheila.

"I don't 'have' anyone," Sheila says. "You may try to possess someone, but you never really can. It's like we're all a bunch of birds in a dark room, flying into each other now and then, but never flying in the same direction with some other bird. We just keep flitting about looking for an exit and some light. It's ridiculous. But I could go for a new relationship right now. An affair, a fling, something to get some excitement back in my life. Because the excitement is gone with Roy—Roy is my boyfriend," she says to me—"and I've been thinking about calling it off."

Lisa says, "Two weeks ago you told us you and Roy went to a hotel room and messed around like crazy and you loved it."

"That was two weeks ago," Sheila says. "And yes, we did fuck our brains out, and yes, I did love it, but it was shallow. It didn't mean anything."

"Does it always have to mean something?" Tasha asks.

"It can be meaningful to fuck your brains out. The sex was great. But it happened two weeks ago. I should dump Roy, but I don't want to until there's someone else in the picture to take his place. Jesus, listen to me. I'm getting too old for this. I need to marry someone."

"That's cruel," Amelia says.

"Getting married?"

"What you said about Roy."

"I know, but that's me. That's who I am. I don't like being alone."

None of us do, I think.

"The problem is," Sheila continues, "finding a new man."

"There are men everywhere," Cara says.

"But the majority of them aren't ones you want to jump in bed with," Sheila counters. She nods toward the bar. "Like that man there. He has a nice profile. He has a nice build; I like the way he wears his suit. I like the tint of gray in his hair; it gives him style in a Richard Gere-sort of way. Look at the way he stands: He looks confident, and he looks like he'd be a good fuck."

"How can you know that from one look?" Lisa asks.

"I don't know, but I'm usually right. I'm not the type of person who finds men in bars, even a nice place like this, but I've had my eye on him for the last five minutes. If I had another drink in me, I might go over there and talk to him."

A blonde in a dark, low-cut evening dress comes up to the man Sheila is talking about. We're all watching. The blonde kisses him, they laugh at something.

"He's taken," Cara says.

"Yes," Sheila says. "And don't they seem comfortable with each other, as if they've been together for a long time?"

"They're probably married," Amelia says.

"I don't think so. He has a wedding band, but she doesn't."

"Observant," Tasha says.

"You think he's cheating on his wife?" Amelia asks.

"He could be separated from his wife," Cara says.

"Then why would he wear the ring?" Sheila says.

"Well, even if he is cheating on his wife," Amelia says, "why would he be wearing the ring?"

"Maybe she knows," Lisa says, "and doesn't care. Some women like to be with married men. There's a certain thrill attached to doing it with someone who's taken. Also, it's safe. No ties. Just sex."

"That's what worries me about getting married," Sheila says. "I don't think I could be faithful forever. Sooner or later, I'm going to meet someone. Maybe just a one-shot deal. But sooner or later I'm going to sleep with someone behind his back. What a dreadful thing to admit to yourself," she adds.

"Or you could have a threesome maybe," Amelia says. "Then there are no secrets, it's out in the open."

"The age of swingers is over," Cara says. "I think it was over before we were even born."

"It died in the early eighties, really," says Sheila. "You can't do that sort of thing anymore."

I think of Veronica.

"Very few people are faithful anymore," notes Lisa, dipping a finger into her wine glass, then sucking on it. "Take my father, for example. He was always having affairs."

"And you knew?" Amelia says. "Did your mother know?"

"She knew. The family knew."

"Did they get a divorce?" from Tasha.

"No. They're still together."

Cara says, "Your mother knew he was having affairs, but she stayed with him?"

"She loved him. Still loves him."

"That's love?"

"Yes—you don't understand," Lisa says, sounding frustrated. "Just because my father did that didn't mean he'd fallen out of love with my mother. Things are better now. He's not chasing women anymore; at least I don't think he is. There was a time when I thought they would divorce. There was a lot of turmoil. My parents were fighting, and sometimes physically, not just with words. There was a time I thought I would go crazy. Maybe I was crazy.

"I was eighteen. We've all been through those confusing years, the mid- and late teens, where you don't know what's going on, you don't know what the world is. You think the world is going to come down on you and sometimes it does. I was drinking a lot then. My father was—is—a drinker, and there was a well-stocked bar in the house. I guess I was drinking too much, too. Alcohol was such an easy and good way out. I called it The Warmth. I loved the way it first hit you, got into your blood stream, went to your head, numbed you all over. I don't drink like that anymore—I keep to wine—but then I was into the hard stuff, gin and bourbon, anything strong that could get me bombed, and bring me The Warmth. I had that romantic notion about alcohol and writing. I was only writing poetry back then, and like most young women writing poetry, my idols were Sylvia Plath and Anne Sexton.

"When I look back on that period, I try to find the point when I told myself things had to change, that I had to stop drinking so much. I think the pivotal moment—and as a writer I guess I'm always looking for pivotal moments—is the night my parents really started to fight and I ran away, not really ran away from home, but ran away from the fight, ran away from it all, because I knew that if I stayed there I would lose my mind completely. I was napping in my room, and I heard them yelling at each other, the same sort of stuff, but with an edge—it was worse this time. I'd been drinking. I jumped up from my nap, hearing my parents yelling at each other from the other room. 'I know,' I heard my mother say, 'I know for a fact that this time, this time—' and I heard my father say, 'You don't know anything.' His voice was calm. 'You're letting your imagination get to you, your insecurities—' he said, and then my mother screamed, 'Goddamn you, I know!' and I heard glass breaking, and then the sound of flesh on flesh—but who hit who?—and there it was again, my mother screaming, my father grunting, and again I heard the sound of glass breaking.

"I ran out of my room and saw my parents on the floor, as if they were wrestling, my mother's lip bleeding, my father's face scratched, and I saw my father raise his hand and hit my mother. He said, 'You bitch, you bitch.' I thought this was a nightmare. I couldn't believe they were being violent with one another. I shrieked and slammed my fist against the wall. My parents stopped and looked at me, with my hand bloody and swollen. My father looked embarrassed and quickly moved away from my mother. I could tell he was drunk, and so was my mother. I was shaking. I thought I was going to combust, just blow up, get rid of the hellish thing I called my life.

"'Go back to your room, honey,' my mother said. My father wouldn't look at me; he straightened his hair and said for me to do as my mother said. I screamed, 'I can't take this bullshit anymore!' and walked out of the house. Well, I ran. My mother yelled 'Wait, wait! Lisa!' but I ran to my car. I had this little Honda Civic at the time; I got in, slammed the door. The keys were in it, I always kept the keys in it. I know that was a dumb thing to do, but I did a lot of dumb things back then. I started my car and drove away."

Amelia says, "Sometimes you just have to do that, you have to get into your car and drive away. I've done that."

"I didn't know where I was going," Lisa says. "I wound up driving to the beach. I parked the car. I went walking in the sand. It was windy—too much wind—my hair was tangled all over my face. A guy in a VW was yelling at me from the parking lot. 'Hey!' he was saying. 'Hey!' I ignored him. 'Hey, sexy!' he called to me. I went back to my car. I looked in the glove compartment and found part of a joint. I lit it. It wasn't good pot, but I never liked pot that much anyway. Eva, my best friend at the time, had left it in there. I found some change in the glove compartment and knew I had to call Eva. I got out, went to a phone booth on the boardwalk, and called her. I heard loud music in the background, lots of guitars.

'Hey,' she said, 'what's up?'

'Things suck,' I said.

Eva said, 'I'm supposed be working on some stupid paper for my government class. I don't think I'm ever going to go to college. Where are you? Outside? I hear sounds.'

"'The beach,' I said.

"'Really?'

"I told her about my parents and she said, 'Oh, that does suck.'

"The guy in the VW drove by me again. He yelled, "Hey, you! Hey, sexy!'

"'Cruise over,' Eva said, 'I know about this party.'

"The guy in the VW yelled, 'Hey, sweetness! Hey, honey!'"

I find the way she tells her story fascinating, with so much detail. But Lisa is, I remind myself, a novelist.

"I told Eva I would be there and ran to my car, afraid of the VW guy. He followed me from the street to the freeway. He was closing in on me from behind, flashing his brights. I started to drive fast. I swerved through traffic and lost him as I exited onto another freeway to get to Eva's. I could hear his voice in my head: 'Hey, girlie. Hey, sexy.'

"All over Eva's bedroom walls were posters and cut-out ads of male models: dark skin, rippling abdominals, shapely chests and arms, chiseled chins, slicked-back hair, blue and green eyes. 'Of course,' Eva always liked to say when she pointed at them, 'this isn't what you really get in a guy.'"

Unconsciously, I sucked in my gut, then stopped when I realized what I was doing.

"I didn't have anything to wear to the party," Lisa continues. "So we hunted through the jungle that was Eva's closet. We were the same size, pretty much. We stripped to our underwear—I didn't have a bra—I'd left the house without one—and we stood in front of the full-length mirror on her wall. Call it 'Portrait of Two Bodies.' We mixed and matched various fabrics, pranced and strutted. Eva was really skinny; she was bulimic, never took in a decent meal, but of course thought she was fat. 'I'm fat,' she'd say, patting the white skin on her flat stomach.

"I decided on black slacks, knee-length boots, and a red blazer, with just a bra underneath," Lisa says, looking a bit coy. "Eva went with a black bodysuit and gray overcoat.

"The party was in the valley. I didn't know any of the people. Eva really didn't either, but that never bothered her; she was quick with the friendly chat and the glad-to-meet-you smile. It wasn't in me to be so gregarious. I said hi to people I didn't know and felt dumb. I went to the makeshift bar to get a drink. A strong drink. I needed a drink. I finished it and got another, then another, and another, all within an hour. I figured, Hell, it runs in the family, right? I saw Eva off in a corner talking to a guy in a nice jacket. She still had the same drink she'd started off with. I kept drinking. Somewhere along the line, I got to a phone and called my mother. I saw Eva in her corner pressed between two guys in nice jackets. I think I may have been on my seventh drink by this time. My mother answered the phone.

"'Mommy?' I said.

"Her voice sounded worried: 'Where are you?'

"'This place,' I said, 'a party.'

"'I was worried about you,' she said.

"I told her I was with Eva.

My mother said, 'Your father left, I don't know where he went.'

"I asked, 'What's going on between you two?'

"'This time I caught him,' my mother said. 'I surprised him with Tammy, a girl he hired at the store—' She stopped, then added, 'I probably shouldn't be telling you this.'

"I couldn't believe," Lisa says, "how matter-of-factly she told me this. It made me hot in the chest. My own father, cheating on my own mother! I knew he was doing this before, though, so why should I be surprised? Why should my mother be surprised? I wasn't listening to what my mother was saying; her voice was soft, she was going blah-blah-blah.

"I felt strange. My mother said 'Lisa, are you okay?' but I just hung up the phone. I got a refill, a stronger drink this time. The music at the party was getting too loud. There were so many people, so much laughter, talk, talk, giggle, giggle. Eva stumbled over to me and said she said thought some guy put something in her drink; she said she was tripping, seeing trails and little dragons all over.

"'Happy happy,' Eva whispered.

"One of the guys in the nice jackets grabbed her arm, pulled her to him, and kissed her. Eva laughed and said, 'Oh, hiya!' and I just figured she was having a good time."

Lisa sips her wine, says, "I met this guy there. I don't know where he came from. 'Smile,' he said to me. He was tall, he smelled nice, and he was older—not that much older, but—but anyway, I looked at him and said, 'Huh?'

"'You have a scowl on your face,' he said. 'Smile and make it go away.' So I did.

"The next thing I know, he was kissing me, this smiling guy, and he had his hands under my blazer, and he was touching me, my breasts, my stomach. He was kissing my lips and eyes, saying nice things to me. I touched his crotch, I felt him, felt something warm, and I was thinking of Eva, but I knew Eva was with some guy, too.

"And then we were walking away. Walking out of the house. Bye-bye party. I leaned into this guy I didn't know because I was having trouble walking."

Listening to Lisa talk, I fall into the trance of her story. I don't know if it's me or her. But I see myself as the man, the stranger, she is with. I know I am he. I want to be him. I'm with her at the party and she's drunk, so I take advantage of this; I've been with younger women like her, who get drunk, and so I make my move. I kiss her and she doesn't object. I touch her and she doesn't object. My hands are under her jacket. She has smooth warm skin. She is touching me. I don't live far from here so I take her away from the party, I take her home. She's drunk; I have to help her walk. Home isn't too far. I've done this before. And as Lisa talks, I see it all so clearly, the two of us: I am this man, because I'm all men.

CHAPTER 6 . . .

It's morning and I'm kissing the back of her neck: Lisa's neck. She stirs; I see her look at her watch. She's naked. She realizes she's not in her bed, but she's with me. She's probably thinking, Who's that at my neck? I say, "So Sleeping Beauty is awake."

I kiss her mouth, which is dry. I'm naked. My erection is pressed against her. I get on top of her. She can't move. She's numb. I push her legs open, touch her down there. I see recognition in her eyes, that she knows who I am: the guy at the party, the smiling, kissing, leaning-into-you guy. Before she can say anything I'm inside her, fast; I know I hurt her a little, but realize I have to move fast if I want another lay; she might change her mind. I'm probably older than she thought I was. I'm in my late-thirties, have a few strands of gray in my hair. I put my face into her chest, her warm breasts, and fuck.

She closes her eyes and probably tells herself she isn't going to enjoy this. She's probably wondering if we had sex last night, probably doesn't remember. She isn't sure, she was so drunk. But we did have sex. The bed is shaking, the mattress springs are making sounds. I say, "Yes, yes." Her clothes are on the floor and I know she's looking at them. The floor is bare and wooden. There are paintings on the walls. I fuck her faster, I groan, I come inside her, I fall on her, breathing hard. I grab her face, lightly kiss her lips, and say, "Good, good."

I get out of the bed. I take off the condom and toss it to the floor—where there are two others. I see Lisa look at them; she probably wonders if the condoms are from last night. Yes, I want to tell her, they are. I go to the closet and put on a pair of black sweats. I ask her if she wants breakfast. She says she doesn't know. "I'm going to make some breakfast," I say, and leave the room.

CHAPTER 7 . . .

"I got out of the bed," Lisa tells us, "and picked up my clothes from the floor. I dressed real fast. I looked at myself in a mirror by his CD player. My make-up was smeared, my hair was a mess, and my face looked a bit puffy. I thought I looked awful and wondered why he even wanted to have sex with me. This had never happened to me before—a one-night stand with a stranger, a hangover that bad. In fact, I'd only had sex with two guys before that—both boyfriends, both I thought were serious relationships at the time, that was the only reason I made love with them. I had never, ever had sex casually before. Those two boyfriends, like my father, had left me for the comfort of other women, and that's why they never became all that serious.

"I left the bedroom. This man, whose name I still didn't know, was cooking eggs and bacon in the kitchenette. The apartment's furnishings were minimal—a black couch, a shelf of books, Arabic-style paintings on the wall, a card table with a small computer.

"He made breakfast for us both. I was hungry, I was numb, I was curious, so I sat with him on the floor and ate breakfast with him. I sat a distance from him and we ate in silence. I told him I was thirsty. 'Help yourself to the fridge,' he said.

"I went to the fridge. There was milk, soda, juice, and beer. 'Can I have a beer?' I asked."

"With a hangover?" from Amelia.

"Sometimes it's the best thing," Sheila says.

"He felt the same way," Lisa says.

"'So early?' he said, laughing.

"'Yeah,' I said.

"'Well, if you want, sure,' he said. I came back with the beer, opened it, sat down, drank it, ate the breakfast. He got up, sat on the couch, and looked at me.

"'Can I use the phone?' I asked.

"'Sure, be my guest,' he said. I called my mother.

"She picked up on the first ring: 'Lisa?'

"I said, 'Yes, yes, it's me.'

"She said, 'Where are you?!'

"I said, 'I'm okay.'

"She said, 'I was so worried about you!'

"I said, 'I'm all right.'

"'Lisa, honey,' she said.

"I said, 'What?'

"She said, 'Your father.'

"'Daddy?'

"'He may not come home,' she said. 'He's with—Tammy. That woman.' And then my mother proceeded to tell me that my father might move in with this woman, Tammy, and live with her.

"'I hate that bastard,' I said.

"'Don't say that,' my mother said.

"'He's a terrible husband!' I said.

"She said, 'But I still love him.'

"'But Mommy,' I said, 'even if he's with her?'

"My mother told me that he was her first love, first and only, that they had met when she was sixteen and he was twenty-six, and she'd never been with anyone before then, or since. 'Things will somehow work out,' she said.

"I felt sick. I told Mommy I had to go. She said my name over and over and I said bye and hung up. I seemed to be hanging up on her a lot those days.

"When I put the phone down, this stranger whose home I was in, this stranger I'd had sex with several times although I only remembered this morning, laughed at me. I looked at him. He said, 'Mommy? Did you say Mommy?' I didn't know what he meant. He said, 'And Daddy, too?' I made a face. I asked what his name was.

"'You don't remember?' he replied.

"'No,' I said.

"'Waite.'

"'Oh.'

"'And you're Lisa.'

"'Yes.'

"'How old are you?' he asked.

"'Eighteen.'

"'Eighteen,' he said. 'Mommy and Daddy.'

"A wave of alcoholic nausea was coming over me. I said, 'Are you making fun of me?'

"'Oh, no,' he laughed. 'Not me!'

"'How old are you?' I asked him.

"He hesitated before saying, 'Thirty-seven.'

"I asked him if I could have another beer. He nodded and asked me to bring him one, too. I did. We drank the beers. He said, 'It's been years since I've started the morning with a drink. You're a bad influence on me, Lisa.' I sat cross-legged on the floor and stared at him. I knew I was making him self-conscious. He said, 'What?'

"'How did we get from the party to here?' I asked.

"'You don't remember?'

"'I remember a little,' I said, and that was the truth. 'Very little,' I said.

"He said quickly, 'You wanted to come here, I didn't force you.'

"'I remember you told me to smile,' I said. 'That's how we met.'

"He said, 'You seemed sad, or angry, pissed off, frustrated at the world.'

"'Yeah, all of the above,' I told him.

"'What happened?' he said. 'Was your boyfriend mean to you?'

"'I told him I'd had a friend with me. I came to that party with a friend, and I asked him if he had seen her. 'She was this girl—' I started.

"He said, 'Hell, there were a lot of girls there, and you happened to be one of them. The lucky one,' he added. The bastard.

"I used his phone again, this time to call Eva. There was no answer. 'Maybe I should go,' I said, and looked at the door.

"'Wait,' said Waite, 'you don't have to go.'

"I wasn't sure what to do.

"He asked, 'Do you feel uncomfortable?' I nodded. He said he could understand that. But I said I really should go. 'Wait,' said Waite, 'maybe we can get together again, have a real date? Like dinner? A movie? Something. Can I call you?' I gave him a number, but it was a wrong number.

"So I started to go but—

"'Wait,' said Waite."

Amelia giggles.

"He asked me if I wanted to go to the bedroom," Lisa says, "and fool around some more. I couldn't believe he was asking me such a thing. 'Another round for the road,' he said. I said no, and went to his door and opened it.

"But I stopped. I turned around. He was standing, and now he had a smile on his face. He probably thought I had changed my mind. But I didn't know where I was. I asked him where the house the party had been was. My car was there.

"'Oh,' he said, 'it's just down the block. It's big, you can't miss it.' And so I left. I heard him say, behind me, 'Bye.'"

"Ah," Sheila says, "you should have had him one more time."

"Or he have you," Tasha says.

Sheila says, "Well, he was good-looking, right? You wouldn't have gone anywhere with him in the first place if he wasn't, drunk or not, right?"

"I just wanted to get out of there, away from him," Lisa says. "I didn't want to go home. I didn't know where I wanted to go. It was a clear morning. The sun was out, et cetera. The house was two blocks down. My car was still there. I felt so relieved. Eva was in the back, curled up, asleep. I knocked on the window. Eva got up and got out; she looked bad. She said, 'What the hell happened to you?'

"I said, 'You wouldn't believe it,' and then I noticed this black mark, a bruise, on Eva's cheek. I asked her about it. She touched it and said, 'Oh. Shit.'

"We got into the car and drove away. Eva opened the glove compartment and looked in, and said, 'Where's that joint I left in here?' I told her I'd smoked it. We got on the freeway. Eva said, 'This guy I was talking to put XTC in my drink.' She stared out the window, then said, 'He seemed really nice, despite that. That drug made me so—hot. God, I wanted him. So he took me into this room, but there were these two other guys there. I tried to get away. They just laughed. They threw me on the bed. Over and over, they took turns.

"'What?' I said.

"'They did everything,' Eva said. She started to cry.

"'Do you want to go to the hospital? Do you want to call the police?'

"'No,' she said. 'Just take me home.'

"'Okay,' I said. After I dropped her off, I went home myself. Mommy wasn't there. At the door were some roses waiting. They were from Daddy, for me. A card said: 'Flowers for my flower. Please don't be mad at me, honey. I love you.'

"I took a shower, dressed, and I drove down to the mall where my father's store was. I watched him from outside, watched him talk and laugh with two of his female employees. He was being flirtatious. I wondered if he was sleeping with one of them, or both? And where was this Tammy?

"I left. I drove around. I stopped and got gas. I called my mother. Mommy answered, but I hung up. What did I have to say? What could I say? Writer though I supposedly was, I could think of nothing to say. I called Eva; there was no answer. I drove to a liquor store and looked at the selections. There was a short old man behind the counter. I told him I wanted a pint of bourbon. He looked at me and said, 'You old enough to buy this stuff, missy?' I said yeah. He asked for ID. I got out my fake ID, which I had had since I was sixteen, and slammed it down on the counter. 'Okay, okay,' he said defensively, and sold me the pint of bourbon.

"I sat in my car and turned on the radio. I opened the bottle. Drank. It stung. I forced myself. I drank nearly half the pint, very fast, feeling it burn down my throat. I sat back, eyes closed, and listened to the music. Quickly, the Warmth spread from my stomach to my blood, bones, and brain. This is better, I thought. I feel much better."

"Hey, look who's here," Amelia says.

CHAPTER 8 . . .

"Holly," Amelia says. "Ms. Late. In the flesh."

We all turn to look. A slender Asian woman with jet black hair in a dress and overcoat approaches the table. She smiles and says hello to all and they say hello back. She looks at me.

I nod, ready to explain my presence, but Amelia does it for me, saying, "This is Leonard; he's Tasha's ex-hubby."

"Well," Holly says.

Amelia moves into the booth and Holly sits by her. I notice Holly has wider eyes than most Asian women and wonder if she's fully Asian.

Tasha waves for the waitress.

Holly looks at me and says, "You must feel gauche."

"Not at all," I say.

"Or lucky," she says. "How many men wouldn't kill for the chance to be with six such wonderful women?"

"Here, here," from Sheila.

The waitress comes by. More rounds are ordered. I notice Lisa looking down at something, nothing, then look up. I wish I knew what she was thinking about. I want to ask how Eva is, if she ever ran across Waite again.

"Sorry I'm late," Holly says. "Again."

"Again," Cara says, smiling.

Holly says, "But we found out who's been sending me all that e-mail. We finally caught the bastard."

"You did?" says Sheila.

"Someone's been harassing Holly on-line," Tasha tells me. "It's been going on for a while."

"I don't have e-mail," I say.

"He doesn't even have a computer," Tasha says.

"I got a late start on the information superhighway," I say.

"Well," Holly starts.

"So what about this guy who's been sending you the e-mail?" Cara says.

"You don't want to get Holly started on the information superhighway thing," Amelia says to me. "She'll never shut up."

"Well, this guy," Holly says, "turns out to be the system administrator of our computer network!"

"What?" says Sheila.

"At your work?" Tasha says.

"The very one," Holly says.

"I thought he was helping you catch the guy," Lisa says.

"That's probably why we couldn't figure out who he was."

I ask, "What kind of e-mail was he sending you?"

"He was a pervert," Sheila says. "And even if I do like perverts," she grins, "this guy is, was—is a jerk."

"Sexually harassing stuff, mostly," Holly tells me. "What he wanted to do to me: rape, bondage, the usual garbage."

I don't know what the usual garbage is.

Holly says, "We knew whoever was doing it had to have known a lot about system networking and hacking. The headers of his e-mail gave no origination routes, so there was no way to trace where they were coming from. I had a feeling it was someone in the company, because the guy knew how I dressed, what my schedule was—so I knew it wasn't somebody off the net, like from one of the Usenet groups I post to now and then. I would look at the men in my office and wonder, 'Are you the one?' The thing is, Mr. Huegen, the sysop who was doing it, is a quiet, nice fellow. Tall and thin, wears glasses, acts shy."

"The perfect neighbor-next-door," Sheila says, "turns out to be a psycho-killer on America's Most Wanted, and everyone is shocked—'Oh, he was the perfect, quiet neighbor.'"

"Yeah," Holly says, "I know."

"That's insane," Amelia says.

"I feel like such an idiot," Holly says.

"Don't," Tasha tells her. "How could you have known it was him?"

"I told Huegen how much these letters were bothering me, that I was scared, and he seemed so sincere, as if he understood. But—"

"—he was secretly laughing about it," Cara finishes.

The waitress returns, placing the drinks down.

"Boy, do I need one of these," says Holly, drinking half of it with one drag on the straw. "What a day—but I don't want to talk about it. What were you kids chatting about before I got here and what do you"—she looks at me—"think of all this?"

"Drinking," Amelia says, "Lisa's drinking."

"It's interesting," I say.

"Or when she used to be a drinker," Amelia adds.

"I bet," I say, and I'm not sure I understand Holly's glare. Her eyes are too dark, and so is this bar.

"We're all drinkers right now," my ex-wife says.

"The first time I got really drunk—and it was my first time ever drinking anything—I was, I think, thirteen," Cara says. "It was gin. Things were spinning everywhere. I puked all over the place."

"Did you do anything bad?" Sheila asks.

"Nah. I was inside, alone, at home, and bored, and I wanted to try the gin my folks had out. From that day until now, I can't drink gin."

"Maybe I'll order a gin and tonic next," Sheila smiles.

Lisa still stares at her wine glass; I still want to know what she's thinking.

"I don't think I've really ever gotten drunk-drunk," Amelia says. "At least not to the point where I've gotten out of control or sick."

"You must've at one time," Sheila says. "We all have at one time or another."

I think about Tasha, and Veronica, and other times

later, drinking, Tasha and I hitting each other during a fight.

"I've lost control before," Amelia says, "but not from drinking."

"Drinking is often a way to try and find control," Lisa says, and I'm happy she's speaking again. "But that's a lie you tell yourself," she adds.

"I know about lies," Amelia says. "I know about married men who sleep with other women, too. I slept with a married man once—well, many times. I loved him—I lusted for him, and I couldn't help it. I was even living with another guy, Nick. Have I ever told you about Nick? I don't think so. He was only around for a while. I should say he was living with me since he moved into the place I'd had for a while. And it all had to do with this married guy I was seeing, David.

"I met David when I was still in college, fighting my way through the system to get a degree so I could do what I'm doing now: putting a lot of hours into teaching kids and getting paid crap. But anyway, I met David and was attracted to him immediately. I saw his wedding ring, but thought to myself, 'I don't care, I want him.' And I knew I wanted him when I realized he felt the same way about me and wasn't going to tell me, I'm married.' I don't know what the deal with his wife was. I knew later on, but that's almost a different story–but maybe it isn't a different story. So yes, I slept with David, many times. I was so caught up in my school work, and the men–boys, really–I was meeting, didn't interest me. Immature, most of them. But not David.

"David was twenty-eight, but he seemed older. I knew he loved his wife, but deep down he was used to going from woman to woman and his womanizing was hard to let go of; that's why he took me to bed. We'd go to my apartment because we certainly couldn't go to his. Sometimes we'd even have sex in my car or his and that was pretty exciting. Excitement—I guess that's what it was about. Exciting for him, sure, to cheat on his wife; exciting for me because I knew it wouldn't, couldn't, last, and I never knew when it was going to end. But how can something end if it doesn't have a beginning? For us, there never was a beginning. We just were. Or maybe there was a beginning, because it all led to something else. It led to me meeting The Astronaut."

"The what?" Tasha asks.

"I'm getting to that, and I'm getting to how I became Amnesia. Let's say the beginning starts when I came home, when Nick was living with me. I come home from school and there he is, lounging on the couch, drinking beers. He liked to drink lots of beers. He didn't have a beer-gut, thank God, but when I looked at him, right then, I looked at him and wondered. He was a nice-looking guy, don't get me wrong, but he was pretty blank up here," she points to her head, "maybe like that football player you knew, Lisa—or so I thought at the time. He was sitting there watching TV, but I didn't hear it—all I heard was the clock on the wall. I had—still have—this big clock, and it ticks real loud, I mean loud, tick tock tick tock tick tock goes my clock. That's all I could hear—that clock—as I sat down next to Nick and looked at him. We didn't say anything to each other. He didn't even look at me, just went on drinking his beers and watching the TV as I heard the clock going tickety-tock. I couldn't stand it anymore, had to do something, say something. So I said, 'Hey—'

'Yeah?" he asked.

'I was thinking—'

'What?'

'I was just wondering—'

Silence on his end.

'Hey, are you listening?'

'Sure.'

I said, 'I was thinking, thinking that—' Wait, I forget where I am."

"You were telling him you were thinking," Holly says.

"Yeah," Amelia says. "Well, I asked him if he knew when was the last time we'd made love. He acted dumb. I said, 'You know, when's the last time we fucked?'

'Watch your mouth,' he said, 'you know I don't like you talking like that.'

I told him how I hated other girls I knew at school talking about all the great sex they were getting—their boyfriends and their suitors and their dates and et cetera. He said, 'What other girls do you talk to? You don't have any friends.' That was dumb—of course I had friends! He asked why didn't they ever come over to the place.

'I don't invite them,' I said. He asked why. I said, 'For one thing this place is a mess.' Nick finished a beer, crunched the can, threw it on the floor, and told me I should clean up the apartment. I told him he should help since he contributed to the mess."

"A messy pig," Cara says.

"He said why should he clean house when he worked? I said I worked, too; it was a part-time job at the library and I had school, but all that was work. He told me about busting his ass at the construction site laying cement all day. I said, 'Yeah, well, that's all you seem to lay.' He tried to argue that it was his paycheck that kept us alive which was a lie since I was doing fine before he moved in, even if my parents did help me out with three hundred dollars every month. I told him he could just fuck himself.

'I should slap you for that,' he said. I extended my chin and said, 'Here, do it,' because at least that would be doing something. I knew he wouldn't, and he didn't. He was a chauvinist pig, but he never hit me. 'Something's not right,' I said to him. 'This isn't the way it's supposed to be,' I told him. 'When I pictured my future self, I didn't see this!' He told me to shut up, he said he was watching TV.

I had to get out. I told him I was going to go. That damn clock ticking so loud was too much! He asked where I was going and I said, 'Somewhere! Anywhere!' 'Where?' he asked. 'Away,' I said. 'When?' he asked. 'Now,' I said. 'Okay,' he said. 'That's all?' I asked. I thought, Screw this, and started out the door. He yelled at me to bring him back some beer. Yeah, right, I thought.

I got into my car and drove. I stopped off at a 7-11 and went to the payphone and called David. I told myself before that I wouldn't—and what if his wife was there? But when he answered, he sounded surprised and happy to hear from me. I told him I wanted to see him and he said sure, so we agreed to meet at a bar we used to go to when we were lovers."

Amelia looks at me and I know that I'm David.

I am, after all, every man.

CHAPTER 9 . . .

I'm David and I meet Amelia at this bar we used to go to when we were lovers several months ago. We kiss when greeting, kisses on the cheek, more like old friends than lovers. I get a gin and Seven for her, a beer for me. We find a booth to sit in. The bar is fairly crowded, people playing pool, drinking and talking. "It's good to have a beer now and then," I say.

She says, "It's good to get out, go somewhere, make connections."

"So," I ask her, "how've you been?"

"I don't know," Amelia says. "Home. Always home. School. Work. Nowhere."

"I'd pretty much given up on you."

"Don't say that," she says, looking at her drink.

"I was really surprised you called."

"I was afraid Elaine would answer."

"I'm glad you called." I touch her hand.

"Me, too," she says timidly.

"I didn't think you would," I say.

"Why?"

"I didn't think you were interested anymore."

"Hey," she says, blushing, "I was always interested—even when you didn't know it. I still am."

"Oh?"

"When I first saw you, you were wearing those same sexy jeans you are now, and I thought, Yeah! That's what I thought."

I look and see that I am wearing torn jeans.

"Wouldn't it be cool if people were like dogs and cats?" I say. "We'd meet, sniff each other's crotches, have sex in some indiscriminate dark alley, or right out in the open."

"We don't need to sniff," she says. "We have eyes for that." Her eyes widen and she looks around.

"I'd like to do that," I say.

"What?"

"Just do it out in the open. On a street, in a park. Everyone could be a witness to it—or maybe a participant."

"You have exhibitionist tendencies?"

"No," I say. "I just want something different. I hate the standards."

"Are you unsatisfied?" she asks.

"Always," I reply. "Everyone is."

"No—not everyone. There are people—"

"Are you?"

"What?"

"Satisfied."

"I don't think I know what that word means," Amelia says.

"Um."

"Hey," she says, "look at that girl over there."

"Which one? There's—"

"The one by that pool table, in the tight, tight, tight black dress."

"Yeah," I say, seeing this girl. "It looks painted on her body."

"Do you think she's satisfied?"

"No."

"But she's so gorgeous."

"Yes."

"She could have any man in the world she wants."

"Possibly. Unless—"

"She probably has a good job," Amelia says, "if she even has to work. Maybe she's a model. She probably has lots of money, from the way she dresses, and that jewelry—"

"Maybe, yes."

"Drives a sports car."

"Maybe."

"She's satisfied," Amelia says.

"Nah," I say.

"Why can't I look like that?" Amelia says. "Why can't I look like her?"

"You look fine."

"Why can't I dress like that?"

"You really want to dress like that?"

"I want a lot of things," she says. "I want a leather jacket like that girl over there has on."

I find the next girl in question. "The leather jacket with all those zippers on it?"

"And I want a motorcycle!"

I start to hum the tune to "Born to be Wild."

She leans forward and whispers, "I want to be fucked all night and come a million times and be drenched in a sea of sweat."

"I think that can be arranged," I say.

She straightens her back. "I want to try bungee-jumping."

"Now that sounds like fun."

"I want—" She thinks about it. "I want a new car."

"No, you don't. Bank loans, payments, credit reports."

"I want a new dog," she says, "a little puppy to replace my old dead dog. I miss my old dead dog."

"I know you do."

"I loved my dog."

"She loved you."

"I wonder what she's doing now."

"Flying around in doggie heaven."

"I miss my life," she says.

"What happened to your life?"

"Dunno. It's not the same, not since Nick moved in."

I smile. "So you live with some guy now."

"He lives with me."

"I'm surprised."

"So am I."

"This relationship seems very sudden," I say. "You and Nick."

"I met him at my summer job. We seemed to get along okay. We went to bed on our second date. The next thing I knew, he'd moved in. We were making love a lot and I liked that and I guess—well, he needed a place and I sure needed help paying the rent."

"Oh. Just a convenience? Half the rent and groceries and a dick to put in you from time to time?

"He doesn't even do that anymore," Amelia says. "He's only been with for two months and already the sex is dead. The Death of Sex! What a bad thought. Yikes. I think life would be horrible.

"Sometimes, yes," I say, drinking.

"But you know."

"I know."

"My parents have been married twenty-five years."

"Quarter of a century."

"They sleep in the same bed, but they don't fuck."

"They did at one time. They made you."

"Well, yeah, they fucked once, maybe quite regularly at some time, but they don't anymore."

"You don't know that for sure."

"It's impossible! I just can't picture my parents doing the nasty. No, no, no—too weird."

"Mine did it all the time. The walls were thin and I could hear them at night."

"They don't even kiss good-bye," Amelia says. "After all these years, it's become a routine for them. If the routine were disturbed, the cards would fall. Life would no longer make sense. Weird and bizarre things could happen. I don't ever want to wind up like that."

"Then don't."

"I have to watch my step."

"Things could creep up on you."

"Grab you and gobble you up," she nods. "Then you're really trapped!"

"A victim."

"No way out."

"No escape."

"A narrow passage."

"The clock keeps ticking," I say.

"God, I really do miss my dog," she says.

"Get another."

"I don't know if I want another pet."

"How about a fish?"

"Maybe a fish."

"Get a fish."

"I hate fish."

"Elaine and I have a fish," I say. "It's a really big ugly fish with huge bug-eyes and it just sits in the water doing nothing but being a big ugly fish with huge bug-eyes sitting in the water doing nothing."

"Listen—"

"Yeah?"

"I want to say," she says, "I'm sorry."

"Sorry? For what?"

"I was kind of rude to you the last time we talked."

"Yes," I say, "you were just a little bit rude."

"I didn't know what to say to you. With Nick moving in."

I nod and say, "Every time I called or saw you, you brushed me off."

"I didn't mean anything by it. I guess—I was a little embarrassed."

"Why?"

"About Nick."

"You jumped into it too fast," I tell her. "Not the best thing to do when you feel lonely. When you're needy. It's not a remedy. Not always. Once in a while, maybe."

Silence. Amelia looks around the bar, then says, "Hey, that girl!" She points. "She got up and went to the bathroom and left her leather jacket right on that chair with no one around to watch it for her."

"So?"

"No one's around."

"Yeah."

"I want a jacket just like that one."

"Um."

"I would do anything for a jacket like that," she says.

"Oh?"

"Well, heck, I could just go over there and take it and leave the bar quickly and no one would probably notice."

"Ha!"

"I could."

"You could."

"I should."

I say, "There are no rules when obtaining something you really want."

"Or need."

CHAPTER 10 . . .

"I took it," Amelia says, smiling and sipping her beer.

"You what?" Lisa says. "You took the leather jacket?"

"Yep."

"You stole it!" Sheila laughs. "I love it!"

"You didn't," Tasha says.

"I did," Amelia nods. "We got outta there fast, laughing and scared. I was giddy with the adrenaline rush. I was a thief—a leather jacket thief! We both had our cars there, but we took mine—mine was the closest—and we got out of there. And what with all the excitement, of course I wanted him, I knew I wanted him, and so we went back to my place."

"But Nick was there, wasn't he?" Cara asks.

"Yeah, that's what he asked me. I told him Nick was asleep by now. I'm not sure why I wanted to take David to my apartment. We couldn't go to his—and we could've gotten a room, I guess, or fuck in my car, but I wanted him in my home. After all, it was my home and I could do whatever I damn well pleased, right? Maybe I just wanted Nick to see him, and Nick did. It's weird.

"Okay, we get to my place and Nick's asleep so we're quiet as we go in. David wondered if we'd wake him. I said, 'Nothing wakes him; he's probably dead drunk.' I was embarrassed how my place was a mess. David said something about it; I just said I was sorry. What could I do? I lived in squalor and now I was presenting it to my former lover, who would now be my lover again.

"It started innocently, if anything ever starts that way. We turned on the TV, kept the volume low, searched the channels. There was a steamy movie on HBO with a sex scene, and that got me started. I was so—um," she looks at me and shrugs, "horny. We got close. He knew I was tense, so he began to massage me. Like they say one thing led to another and we made love. We lost sense of where we were. We must have been loud, because the next thing I knew, Nick was watching us."

"Oh?" Sheila raises a brow. "Watching?"

Tasha had watched me and Veronica.

"He didn't stop us, didn't interrupt," Amelia goes on. "He just stood in the dark and watched us do it. I didn't know. I was so caught up in the good sex. I needed the sex. And when we were done we were there on the floor for a bit and Nick finally came out and said, 'Well, I guess hello and greetings are out of order.'"

"You're joking," Cara says.

"I'm not! He really said that! Scared the hell out of me! I jumped up and grabbed my clothes, like he was a stranger, like he'd never seen me naked before, and began to put my clothes on, even the leather jacket. David, however, didn't react—he was just casual and cool about it. He sat up and said, 'Hey, what's up?'"

Sheila laughs.

Amelia says, "I was frantic. I started putting it together that Nick knew, that he'd been watching."

"Interesting," from Sheila.

"I asked him how long he'd been there and he said the whole time and I just couldn't believe it. I said, 'You watched?!' and David seemed amused by it all."

"I would have been, too," Sheila says.

"But Nick was acting as if David wasn't even there. He looked at me and said, 'Where'd you get that jacket?' and I told him it was mine and he said, 'You don't have a jacket like that,' and I said, 'I do now.' Then David said, 'She stole it.' I could've killed him. But I admitted it, I told Nick I did steal it. Nick said, 'Who is this guy?' but he didn't look at David. He was looking at the floor, then at me, not angry but very confused. 'I don't want this to turn into a scene,' I said to him, and then I told David to get dressed because he looked stupid sitting on the floor in the buff. Cute and desirable, but given the circumstances—stupid."

"This sounds surreal," Lisa says.

"It was," Amelia says. "So David said to him, 'Hey did you really watch us?' as he got dressed and I said to Nick, 'If you did, you're a sicko,' but I didn't know what I meant by that. I mean, well—Nick said it himself, he said, 'I don't believe this! You go out and see this guy and you bring him back here, where we live, and you have sex with him, here, with me here.'"

"I guess you could say that was a little rude," Sheila says, drinking, eyes glinting.

"Nick asked why we didn't go to his place and I said, 'We couldn't.' 'Bad idea,' David said. I said, 'We couldn't because his wife is there.' I wanted to be fully honest, out in the open. What was there to hide? I was sick of secrets.

Nick looked at David and said, 'You're married?' David nodded and said, 'Married two years.' Nick said to me, 'You fucked a married man?' and David said, 'It's not as bad as it sounds,' and I said, 'It's just something that happened,' because what more can you say? I wasn't in the mood to philosophize about morality.

'It's not like we see each other all the time,' David said to Nick, 'in fact I'm as surprised about this as you are. Amelia and I haven't seen each other in a long time.' Nick said rather calmly to David, 'Normally, I would probably kill you, but this isn't normal and I've never been in a situation like this.' He really said that, and it shocked me—I'd never heard Nick talk like that, examining himself in that way, because I was expecting any moment for Nick to attack David and fight with him, and Nick had more muscles, was more Neanderthal in a way, so I was afraid of a scene and wanted to get David out of there as fast as possible, with little or no conflict.

"I told Nick again that I did not want a scene to erupt. David was dressed by then and he said, 'I'm not in the mood for anything harsh.' 'Normally I would,' Nick kept saying, 'I'd just kill you. But it just doesn't seem to be in me. There's no rage, no anger. Only—a numb feeling. I feel hollow. I don't like this feeling, I don't like this at all.' 'You have no frame of reference for it, no way to really process it,' David said. I looked at them both." Her voice lowers. "Something snapped in me. I had this perverse fantasy of having sex with them both. I've never had sex with more than one man, but I could see myself making love to them both, and then the two of them killing each other afterwards. I felt really weird. Nick said to me, 'Amelia, I just want to know why.'

"Then something else snapped in my head," Amelia says. "I don't know what it was. I began ranting, raving, a monologue from hell. I paced around the room. My mouth was just going and it made no sense. I was thinking of my dead dog. I said to Nick—I said to them both, 'Why? I'll tell you something, I'll tell you both something! The week before I moved out of my parents' house and got this apartment, my old dog died. I was jogging and she was with me. She took off somewhere else as I was jogging, just went off in this different direction. It was dark out. She'd done it before, a while back, but she always came back home. This time she didn't, though, and I started to get worried.

"The pound called me the next morning. My dog had been found in the street. Hit by a car, Her tag had my phone number on it. I went down there, to the pound. She was a mess—she was stiff, in an odd shape because her backbone had been broken. I kept wondering how it had happened. The area they found her in—a lot of people jog there. Her eyesight had gone bad and it was dark and I imagined she saw some jogger and thought it was me so ran across the street and that's how she got run over.

"I'd had this dog for years, since my teens. When I was lonely, she was always there. Now I was alone, and even more alone, because she was gone. I cried when I saw her, and touched her body. I hadn't cried in a long time over anything. I had to go down to the pound by myself and pick up her dead body, her stiff and broken dead body and what I really needed then and there was someone to hold me. A man, a boyfriend, someone close. Strong arms and a chest to hold me. But I had no boyfriend at the time, I had no one, so I had to hold myself, and that's a horrible thing. I cried into myself. Never—never had I felt so alone in my life, ever, but then I told myself: This isn't really all that bad—because being alone meant having no obligations, no one to answer to.'"

CHAPTER 11 . . .

"But I wasn't really sure what I meant by all that," Amelia says, finishing her beer.

"So what happened then?" Cara asks. "Did Nick start a fight?"

"No. He just stood there, like a statue. And David and I left."

"Just like that?" Tasha asks. "Nothing else? Nothing bad happened?"

"No. I had to take David back to his car. We didn't say anything much on the way. He asked if I would be okay and I said yes. We promised to get together soon, but it seemed meaningless—as if we never would, as if this would be the end of it. He got into his car and went back home to his wife."

"Was it the end of it?" Lisa says.

"No, no, there's always more," Amelia says. "Things don't end as neatly as they do in TV shows. But anyway—that was it, that's what started it all, that's how I came to meet The Astronaut. I couldn't go back to the apartment. I wanted to get away, I wanted to leave forever. I wasn't thinking. I started to drive, I got on the freeway. I had to get as far away as possible because I knew right then and there that no matter how much I needed or wanted someone to be a part of my life, to be in my life, no matter what, maybe it was best that I just went it alone. The loner: moi. The drifter. The old maid. I didn't care. All I knew was that I had to get the hell away, far away.

"And so I did. I never thought I'd ever be able to do something like that, but there I was, in my car, driving away. I was taking the highway east, out of the city. I was going into the mountains, the desert, I was just driving and driving—and I need another beer," she says, holding her bottle up.

I turn to wave for the waitress because I see that we all pretty much need new drinks, and that's when I see Frederick Slater.

CHAPTER 12 . . .

"I am getting a little drunk," Amelia adds, "but not too drunk."

Tasha sees Slater, too. I don't need to look at her to know this, I feel it from her body, a wave. I know her well enough to pick up on these things; I know her body, something I possessed, or wanted to possess, as much as I wanted to possess Veronica. Slater is at the far end of the bar, talking to a man in a three-piece Perry Ellis suit. Slater's suit is a bit rumpled, his tie loosened, his silver hair neatly slicked back. I believe he's in his mid-fifties, I don't remember. I don't think Tasha ever told me. They'd been lovers once, but from what I know, he's been lovers with many young women in the publishing industry. I'd met him before at publishing parties I had gone to with Tasha, but I didn't know they'd had sex until much later, when she had sex with him while we were married. It happened right after our night with Veronica. She said she didn't know how it happened, it just did, probably much like the encounter Amelia had with David. An act without prologue.

The waitress comes to our table just as Slater and the man he's with leave the bar. He doesn't notice that Tasha is here, or the other women, and doesn't see me, either. I'm glad. When I turn back and look at my ex-wife, I see she's relieved too, judging from the change in her expression, ever so slight, on her face, but—I know her. There is a quick exchange between us. It's in our eyes, we both recognize it: the secret history of something else.

It's probably not something Tasha has disclosed to her friends, despite their apparent candor with one another. In fact, my ex-wife has been rather quiet all this time; I don't know if this is usual for her, or if it's my presence. She has always been a reserved person. She was that way when we first met. She can have her wild moments of grandiloquence and anger; I have seen her lose control on several occasions. Tasha is a woman who takes pride in control, in a world that runs logically; and when that falls apart, so does she. This is one of the reasons why we are no longer together.

The waitress comes by. Only some of us order more drinks. Amelia does, and so do I, and so does Sheila. Holly, Cara, Lisa, and Tasha aren't ready for more. Some people drink, and some people don't.

I'm getting drunk, too. I want to, especially after seeing Slater.

"Married men mean no obligations," Sheila says. "It's pretty cut and dried—it's all about fucking. There's nothing more to it. There isn't a future to think of."

"Not all the time," Lisa says.

"But most of the time," Sheila says. "Although I've told myself: 'No more married men, it's just not right.' That isn't a moral statement; I don't feel any particular obligation to the wife, you understand. It's just not right for me. It's okay to play around with them when you're younger, but now that I'm getting older," she shakes her head, "it's just plain stupid. And I always wonder, if I get married—when, if—will I ever be that other woman, will I be someone's wife in her forties, fifties, whose husband is off having a quick poke with a bouncy twenty-two-year-old?"

Twenty-two. That's the age Tasha was when she met and slept with Slater for the first time. She told me about it two weeks after our night with Veronica. She came home and said we had to talk. The sound in her voice didn't make me feel good. It was a bad night, and it had been a bad day. A man I'd served a summons on in the East Side had come after me with a bat and would've done some damage if I hadn't been quick and dodged him. I was drinking beer and watching TV; Tasha came in, put her briefcase down, and said, "We have to talk." I knew we were reaching the end of something, if we hadn't already.

"I can't lie to you," Tasha told me. "I slept with another man three days ago. In a hotel room, after work—it just happened. It was quick. It was dumb. It's only happened this once and I don't think it'll happen again, but I can't say for sure because I don't know what my life means anymore. I don't know what's happening in the world. I don't know anything."

I just looked at her.

"I didn't do it in retaliation for anything," she said. "That would be too easy. I didn't stop you—didn't stop us—from what happened. I don't blame you, and I don't blame Veronica. I don't even blame myself. But I slept with this man and I guess you should know about it."

"You guess," I said, "that I should know."

"You have a right."

I asked, "You couldn't keep this a secret?"

"Secrets kill you."

That hurt. I said, "Who is he?"

"Frederick Slater; you've met him before."

I couldn't put a face to the name. She mentioned several parties and then I recalled. A rugged, energetic older man—and I didn't have a clue. I never did.

"How?" I said.

"I'm not sure." She didn't look at me—the floor was apparently a better place. "We happened to have lunch," she said, "and we talked about old times, and then we went to a hotel room. It was like I wasn't even really there."

"Old times?"

"We were lovers once," she said. "At least, I was one of the young women he seduced."

"You never told me this before," I said.

"I never told you about a lot of things before," she said. "Leonard."

I nodded.

So she told me. She'd come to the city freshly graduated

from the University of Colorado for the summer publishing program she'd been accepted to, which assured her an entry-level position into the profession she dreamed of. "I was so convinced," Tasha narrated, "that one day I would discover and nurture great writers."

She met Slater during the fourth week of the program, when there were a lot of guest speakers from the industry attending. She came in late, while Slater was speaking. She'd been up till two A.M. the night before, reading, and cursed herself for her tardiness, promising herself to re-adjust her sleeping schedule. She wanted a good start in this field; she felt she needed to motivate herself better.

Slater stopped his lecture when she barged into the class. Slater looked at the clock, then smiled warmly in her general direction. He had the touch. She smiled back, embarrassed. All eyes in the class were on her. Tasha took her seat and Slater continued with his lecture on the mechanics of publishing, from handling writers' manuscripts to dealing with the marketing department. "You want to set your own standards and not fall into the footsteps of others," Slater told the class. To be a great editor you need to make up all new rules that fit into your personal vision of what this damn industry is going to be in the future." He frowned as if to give his own words some thought. Tasha thought he was a handsome man, for his age.

Later that day she saw Slater sitting in a bar near the campus. She was walking down the street and happened to look in the window while passing, and stopped. Was that him? It was. He was alone, with a mug of beer in front of him. She went into the bar, wondering why a man as acclaimed as Frederick Slater was alone. Then again, he was only extolled in the small circle of publishing people and the writers who were hopeful that he'd take them under his wing. She was almost too timorous to approach him, and nearly left the bar; but Slater looked up from his beer and saw her, recognized her, and smiled. Tasha pushed herself in his direction, pulling her black cardigan around her body.

"Hello," he said, looking up.

"Hi."

"Please, sit down, join me," gesturing to the empty chair across from him.

She felt funny, but sat down anyway. Slater had a weary expression. Tasha liked the creases around his eyes and mouth; they were signs of age that signified experience, knowledge, accomplishment—all things she wanted (but not the wrinkles).

She couldn't look at him for long; she had to glance around the bar. She said, "You're alone here." She thought she was acting rather aggressive, which was unusual for her. She knew what she was getting at, she knew what this would lead to—it was all a matter of playing the game. There are always games to play.

"I didn't feel like putting in half a day at the office," Slater said, "and I didn't feel like going home, so I decided to stop here and have a couple of beers."

She nodded. She wanted to ask him how old he was exactly (she would have guessed early fifties), and why he didn't want to go home—she heard he had a place in the best part of the city. She looked at his hands: rough and gentle-looking at the same time. They'd been around, those hands; they'd probably touched many women. She saw he wore a wedding band.

"Can I get you a beer?" Slater offered.

"Sure."

Slater started to get up.

"Wait," Tasha said, touching his arm. "Make that wine, white wine please."

Slater smiled and said, "I didn't think you were the beer-drinking type."

He got himself another mug and a glass of white wine for her and returned. He asked her name. She told him.

"And I bet you want to take Publishers' Row by storm," he said. "Go out and find the new Kerouacs and Updikes. And whomever else."

She didn't know what to say; it was as if he'd read her mind. He'd probably heard the same story many times before.

"If that's what you want, it's advisable," he continued, "to set your standards as high as possible. Never accept anything less than damn good or perfect. Don't go for the mediocre even if it's the only offer on the table. You must always demand the best. How old are you?"

She told him.

"That's a good age," he said, suddenly grabbing her hand. "Twenty-two. And your hands. Such soft hands. Soft, pale skin. You're a lovely young woman, Tasha Ticknor."

She couldn't look at him.

"You don't mind my saying that, do you?"

"No."

His grip tightened. He opened her palm, caressed it. The sensation sent tremors into her, setting off her most remote fears. She didn't know what she was doing, but she didn't want to back off. She had gone this far and she was ready for anything. She imagined herself with this man, naked with him. She hated herself for this—hated her own trepidation. She hadn't had sex with anyone in more than a year.

"Where do you live?" he asked her.

"This summer," she said, clearing her throat, "I'm here on campus, in the dorms."

"Roommate?"

"Single occupancy. Private."

"Will you take me there?" It came out as a mumble as he looked at his beer.

"What?" she said.

He let go of her hand and smiled. "Never mind."

She gaped at her hand and blurted, "Don't stop." She was surprising herself.

Slater laughed. "You must think I'm some dirty old man."

She said, "No."

*****

"All I kept thinking was 'I'm surprising myself, I'm

surprising myself,'" Tasha told me as we sat in our apartment.

"You took him to your room," I said.

She nodded. "I did. There was no time wasted. We both knew . . . in a city like this, it's always rush-rush, never time to play around."

She could taste the beer on his mouth when he kissed her. She was apprehensive at first, then she relaxed. Her year-long hiatus from sexual intercourse was going to end here, and she was glad it would be with this man.

He touched her breasts, feeling the nipples through the fabric of her blouse and bra. "Tell me to stop if you want me to stop," he said. She didn't say a word. She reached to loosen his tie. On the small dorm bed, he caressed her between her legs as she stroked his erection. He moved down and put his mouth to her. She had to let go of his penis and she missed it: she liked having it in her hand; she liked the way it curved; and she thought she would like it in her mouth. He entered her, whispered a few nice things she didn't really hear. She was too caught up in having a man inside her after so long. She let out a hiss as he went in deeper. It hurt a bit, but she had expected it to. After a little while, Slater turned her over on her stomach. He entered her from behind, caressing her buttocks. She came with what sounded to her like a horrible cry, one she knew her neighbors could probably hear. Slater laughed softly, grabbing some of her hair, kissing her on the cheek. "I certainly felt that," he said.

She was trying to catch her breath, saying, "It's—it's—"

"I'll make you come more," he whispered.

Slater moved up, placing his legs on either side of her. He made love to her slowly, gently spreading her ass cheeks with his hands, and rubbing his finger in a spot that made her quiver. He pulled out, spreading the juices of her sex onto her anus. He asked her if she'd ever had sex this way. She told him a few times. He asked if she liked it and she didn't answer. He inserted a finger; she hissed again. With his finger he softly tugged, opening her. She could feel the cold air of the room go inside her. Her skin began to form goose bumps. Slater fit in a second finger, jerking patiently at her flesh; with an experienced tenderness, she thought.

Her body was shaking; his cock was in one place, his fingers in another. He talked to her as he made love to her, saying, "This is nasty, very nasty, Tasha. I always like the nasty side of things. The extremes. But if this were a sex scene in a book—I don't know, I would probably have the writer tone it down some. You can't always give every little detail. But what the heck, eh? Sex is what gets people to buy books these days. Everyone loves to read a vivid, graphic, steamy sex scene now and then."

She was about to say something, but Slater removed himself from her vagina and went into her asshole. She cried out, muffling the sound by biting the pillow. "How is it?" he asked. She mumbled, almost asked him to stop. He fucked her. She breathed deeply. Slater removed himself, went back into her cunt. He did this for a bit, then went back to anal sex. She wondered whether this was healthy or not, then realized she didn't care. "Nasty," Slater moaned, "nasty." Tasha looked at the clock on the nightstand. She watched the clock for nearly forty minutes as Slater went back and forth between her openings, and she reached two more orgasms.

The one she had while he was in her ass was much different than any other, and this was something new for her. Slater turned her around, moved on top of her, his crotch close to her face, offering his glistening member to her mouth. She almost rejected it. He grabbed her hair. She took it, the taste causing her to gag at first. She lay there and let him fuck her mouth. His body spasmed and there was a new taste, his come filling her mouth, warm and salty, flowing easily. He caressed her face and said, "Nice."

"It was dirty sex," Tasha told me as I listened, "but it turned me on. I'd never done anything so dirty and—and I don't know. It got dirtier. Maybe I'm talking too much. I'm sorry, Leonard."

"Go on," I said, even if I didn't want her to. "I want to know everything."

The next day she called the publishing house where Slater worked, asked for his extension.

"Yes—" he said, sounding rushed.

"It's me."

"Who?"

"Tasha Ticknor."

"Oh, yes," he said, and then his voice lowered: "So what can Frederick do for you?"

She thought his referring to himself in the third person was strange. "I thought," she coughed, "I thought maybe we could get together when you get off work."

"Umm," he said, "no, but I will put in a good word for you with personnel."

"A job there?" she said.

"Yes, of course."

"As your assistant?" She perked up.

"No, no, I have one of those. But thanks."

"Oh."

"There are plenty of departments here, plenty of imprints. This is a goddamn conglomerate, as you know."

"Oh," she said, disappointed.

"Look, so much to do, I have to let you go."

She asked, "When—when will we see each other again?"

He said, distantly, "Dear, I'm a married man."

"That didn't seem to concern you yesterday."

"I'll call you," he said.

"You don't have my number here."

"Give it to me."

She recited her number and wondered if he was actually taking it down.

"I could call you later," she offered.

"Do that," he said, and hung up.

She didn't hear from him for a week so she took a day off from the program and went to the publishing house Slater was at. It was near a lot of other publishing houses.

Slater's assistant was a young woman, maybe two or three years older than Tasha. Tasha felt jealous. She wondered if Slater did nasty things with his assistant. She felt awful. Slater agreed to see Tasha, ushered her into his office, although he looked uncomfortable about it. His suit was rumpled.

"You should've called first," he said.

His desk was cluttered with manuscripts, magazines, galleys, other odds and ends. There were boxed and twined manuscripts all around his office. She wondered where he found the time to handle all of it.

"I mean," he added, "I'm always quite busy, but—" He smiled.

"I'm sorry," she said. "I'll go if you want."

"No, no," he said, looking at his desk.

"I was just passing by, I thought—" No, she couldn't lie.

"Why aren't you at the school?" he asked.

"I can afford to miss a day."

"Could be an important day."

"I'll take the risk. I'm a—risky person."

"I'm meeting with an agent for lunch," he told her. "Do you want to come along? It could prove interesting, from the standpoint of your education."

She nodded.

The agent was a man in his thirties. He talked about several of his clients to Slater with fervor. Slater seemed uninterested, but nodded his head and went, "Yes, yes, wonderful, yes, let old Freddy take a look, I'd be happy to." Tasha felt excluded. These men were talking a different language. She started to wonder if she'd ever fit into this business, wondered if she shouldn't just go back to Colorado.

After lunch, the agent shook her hand and said, "I do hope we meet again."

"You should come to my dorm," Tasha suggested in the cab she and Slater shared.

He shook his head. "I have to tell you. The other day— well, last week—was it last week?—was a mistake."

"Why do you say that?" she asked, too loudly. She saw the driver look at her briefly in the rearview.

"Hush," he told her. "I was in one of my moods that day. You were there, so pretty. It was great, my dear, great; you're a marvelous young woman. But I'm a married man, I have two kids in college—well, from my previous marriage, but I have kids almost your age, a daughter who's twenty. Not that that means anything. I love my wife."

"You do this a lot, don't you?"

"What?"

"You like to ravish girls, don't you? Give them one beautiful time and never come back."

He laughed. "I'm hardly the Svengali type."

She bunched up her nose.

"I'd like to see you," he said, "but I can't."

"Can't or won't?"

"No platitudes, please."

She sneezed.

"Come to my home for dinner," he said abruptly.

"Tonight?"

"Tomorrow."

"Why? I—"

"Do you accept or decline?"

"Accept."

"So I went," Tasha said.

"Was his wife gone?" I asked.

"No, she was there."

Tasha took a cab to Slater's uptown condo. He was on the eleventh floor. She knew these were very expensive homes; she thought one day she might own one, too.

She was nervous. She wore a short black skirt and blue blouse, overcoat and scarf. She'd spent an hour on her make-up and hair, wanting to look her best for him, her long legs in black stockings. Slater answered his door. He was in khakis and a turtleneck. She liked him out of the suit. "Ms. Ticknor," he said loudly, "Come in, come in," and he quickly whispered to her, "Follow my lead, play the game."

Always a game.

She nodded, but didn't understand.

A woman came out from another room. Tasha's heart sank; she'd hoped to have Slater all to herself. This other woman was in her early forties; she had a grave air of elegance—Tasha knew she'd come from some well-off bloodline, had probably been educated at Vassar or Sarah Lawrence. So this was Slater's wife, the woman she had to compete with.

"Adrienne dear," Slater said, "this is Tasha—Tasha Ticknor. Our new junior publicist. Ms. Ticknor, I would like you to meet my wife, Adrienne Slater."

Adrienne's grip was firm but feminine. Tasha felt like a child in her presence.

"Ms. Ticknor," Adrienne said. Vassar.

"Nice to meet you," she said, and looked at Slater.

"As I was saying," he said, "Ms.—Tasha here, she's going to be handling some of the promo for my acquisitions, getting those writers, those little rascals, those decrepit scalawags, to their readings and interviews. We'll be working closely together to make sure all my wonderful little storytellers get the attention they so richly deserve."

"So their books will sell," Tasha said emptily. "Sell, sell, sell."

"Yes!" Slater looked pleased; she was playing along.

Adrienne Slater was a marvelous cook. This didn't make Tasha feel any better. No wonder Slater had no intention of leaving this lady. Tasha didn't know how to cook anything beyond a hot dog or a can of soup. The wine she served was rich and strong, and after a few glasses, Tasha's head began to feel light. She actually felt happy, as if she didn't give a damn anymore. She felt she didn't care whether or not she received the affections of Frederick Slater, the worldly lover.

*****

"He led the conversation at the dinner table," Tasha went

on, her voice monotone. "Telling jokes and anecdotes about the publishing business and what he called his 'nasty writers.' 'Those rascals,' he would say of them, some of whom were famous, 'those scoundrels!' He talked and talked and talked, he just wouldn't stop."

"Maybe he was nervous having you there with his wife," I said.

"No. He's always like that. I didn't know it at the time, but maybe he was afraid that his wife would ask me a question I wouldn't be able to answer. She was quiet the whole time; I noticed she looked at her husband with endearment; each time she and I traded glances, she gave me a warm smile."

"She had to have known," I said.

"I don't know; I was getting drunk."

After dinner, they had some more wine. Demurely, Mrs. Slater yawned, said to Tasha she was an early retiree, and that it had been nice meeting her. Mrs. Slater excused herself and went off to bed.

"Tasha and I will be working in the study," Slater called after his wife.

Now she was finally alone with him. He took her to the study. He had an electric typewriter on an old oak desk. There were shelves and shelves of books; hundreds, maybe thousands. Tasha had never seen so many in one room, except in a library. She wondered how many of these books Slater had edited; many bore the imprint of the conglomerate he worked for. She envied him, she wanted to be him. She also wanted to suck him again. She giggled when she thought this, but knew it was true.

Slater sat at his desk. He opened a drawer, produced a bottle of scotch and two glasses; he poured some of the scotch into both.

"Why am I here?" she asked.

"To show you what a great wife I have," he said, "how happily married I am."

"Then why did you fuck me the other day?"

"I needed it. I gather you needed it, too."

"Do you like playing with people's feelings?"

"Look, dear—look, hear, listen, I speaketh," he said. "We both got laid and it was fun. You must leave it at that. I know you're pristine to the city, it's not like that mountain place you come from. But I imagine things are pretty much the same everywhere. If you're going to go into the book business, you must know that this sort of thing happens all the time. You're going to have to get used to it."

"Sleeping around?"

"It's inevitable when people are constantly intermingling. The writers, those darn ruffians, live secluded lives. They write about people, but go without seeing them for weeks at a time. But those of us behind the books are always around people, as you shall see."

"A lot of young women come into this field," Tasha said. "Young women like me. I bet you have quite the pick."

"Here." He held out a glass of scotch.

"I don't usually don't drink hard booze."

"You do tonight, dear."

She was elbowing the seducer again. She took the glass, poured the alcohol down her throat, not thinking. She gagged, coughed.

"Not so fast," Slater laughed, and drank from his own glass.

The effect hit her like a numb slap. Her body tingled, and so did her face. She thought how she would like Slater to take her on his desk, enter her all over, even hurt her if he wanted to.

"I'm too sensitive for my own good," she said.

"What's that?" He took her glass, poured her some more.

"I can't be distant and have sex just for the sake of doing it and nothing more," she told him. "I want meaning."

"Meaning is a good thing to have."

"You've been my first lover in over a year."

"A year?" He looked as if he didn't believe her.

"Yes."

"Are you telling me that in the past year you have had no

desire to sleep with any men? I doubt a beautiful woman like yourself would be lacking in opportunities or suitors."

"I had no desire for anything, really," she said. "Except for books. I love books. I was completely unaware of my physical needs." She crouched before him, her hands on his legs. "Until now," she said.

"Drink this," he said.

"I'm already drunk."

"Drink it," Frederick said.

She snatched the glass and this time the scotch went down smoother. She put the glass on the floor. She ran her hands up and down Slater's legs. He didn't object. She purred. She rested her head in his lap. She could feel the hardness of his erection.

Slater touched her hair gently, but his voice was brash. "Tasha, I want you to suck me off."

She quickly unzipped his pants, tugged at them, then at his underwear, released his cock. It looked bigger than she recalled, but this could have been the alcohol.

What was it with this man? He gets her drunk and talking and then he demands a blowjob like some—scalawag, to use one of his words?

She took him in her mouth. She did, after all, want to eat him. He had a strong smell and taste. She reached under her skirt to touch herself.

Slater was quick. His semen gushed forth like a preacher's sermon, loud and strong. Some of it flowed out of her mouth.

Slater grabbed her head. "Tasha, dear, don't swallow it. Don't ingest my seed. I want you to keep it in your mouth. I want you to keep it in your mouth as long as you can, all night if you can. I want you to swish me around and taste me in your mouth for hours. It means a lot to me. Can you do that for Freddy?"

She had swallowed some, but she nodded.

He pulled her to her feet, his eyes intent and small. "Open your mouth."

She did, showing him she was keeping his essence there.

"I want it there forever," he whispered.

She swished the semen around, got most of it under her tongue; it was easier to manage that way.

"Don't talk," Slater said, and snapped his pants. "Don't say anything. You have to go now."

She frowned.

"You have to go. Go home and go to bed, and keep me in your mouth all night long."

*****

"He showed me to the door," Tasha told me, staring at her feet. "But I saw Adrienne standing in the hall, in a nightgown, looking at us. There was a quick exchange between us and I shivered. She knew. She knew very well what had happened; she knew about all the young women he'd had. I felt dirty, and that's what he wanted: he wanted me to feel dirty, like something bad, like maybe a whore, that was his way of getting rid of me, so I wouldn't come back, so I wouldn't be dirty again. He helped me with my coat and scarf and told me good night, good-bye. He was blasé about it, as if I didn't have his goddamn come in my mouth.

"Outside, it was cold. He hadn't even called me a cab, the asshole. I had to wave one down. When I got into the cab I knew I couldn't do it and didn't want to do it. I didn't want to hold his come in my mouth all night, so I swallowed and told the driver my address and looked out the window. I could still taste him when I got home and the taste didn't entice me any longer because now I knew the truth. I wanted to wash my mouth out a dozen times. I think I even hated him."

"But you went to him again," I said, "and slept with him."

"Not until three days ago."

"And we're married."

"I'm screwed in the head," she told me. "I didn't know what I was doing. I don't know what I'm doing even now."

I felt angry, finally. I had been waiting for that feeling. I asked, "Was the sex dirty? Did you do those things with him?"

"It wasn't dirty," she said. "It was—regular, normal, stupid. I felt stupid, and I think he did as well. I wasn't a fresh conquest, I wasn't as young as before; he was treading old ground and I wanted to do something crazy, because everything seems to be falling apart. You know what I mean, Leonard, but I don't think you understand."

"Are you going to fuck him again?" I asked.

She said, "How do I know who I'm going to fuck anymore?"

I jumped at her and slapped her. There was blood at her mouth. I wanted to taste her blood. I wanted to do something horrible, to remind myself I was real.

CHAPTER 13 . . .

"I used to be a bouncy twenty-two-year-old," Amelia says, "but now I'm not so bouncy."

"Resiliency is the first thing we lose," Sheila says.

"I was twenty-two when I met The Astronaut," Amelia says.

"Astronaut?" Holly says.

Tasha turns, looking at the entrance. I know she's wondering if Slater might come back, and I'm wondering the same thing. "Listen," Tasha says, "we've been here for a long time."

"We're always here," Cara says.

"I know, but do we always have to sit in the same place and same bar?" she says. "Why don't we move about? It's a big city. Since we're being different and have Leonard on our hands, we might as well be different and go somewhere else, maybe several other places."

"Like bar-hopping?" Holly says.

"Yes."

"Hmm," Holly looks around, "we could go somewhere more exciting; this place is kinda dead."

"What do you think?" Tasha asks them all.

"Where will we go?" Lisa says.

"Plenty of places," Sheila says.

Amelia says, "Is Leo coming with us?"

"Well," I look at my drink.

"Only if he wants to," my ex-wife says. "If he doesn't have anything important to do."

"Not really," I say, and I know this isn't the answer she wants, but I'll be damned if I'll give in to her subtlety. "I don't have anything to do."

"Do you want to bar-hop with the girls, Leeeeeooo?" Sheila says, giggling. "Be one of the girls?" She laughs. "I'm sure there are more stories to hear tonight; maybe repeats of stories already told."

"I have to go to the bathroom first," Lisa says.

"Me, too," Cara says.

We all get up from the booth. My knees crack, but it's not audible. I'm getting old.

CHAPTER 14 . . .

"It's such a crowded city," Amelia says, looking out the window.

I'm sharing a cab with Amelia, Tasha, and Sheila. We're crammed in. I'm at one end and Amelia is at the other. Sheila is sitting next to me. Her perfume is expensive and strong. I like the way her hair smells.

There aren't any places near that seem interesting. Sheila suggests a place none of us have heard of. It's a few miles uptown. In the cab behind us are Holly, Lisa, and Cara. I wonder what they're talking about.

"Amelia," Sheila says.

"Yes?"

"You mentioned an astronaut several times before," Sheila says. "Are you saying you did a real live astronaut? Like one who went to the moon?"

"He called himself The Astronaut," Amelia says, "and we went beyond the moon. He went all over the galaxy."

"Girl, you're funny."

"No, really," Amelia says. "I met him right after I decided to run away. Drive away. I had to take David back to his car, of course, but I couldn't go back home. So that was it. It's what made me go and leave, take that car and drive away because I knew right then and there that no matter how much I needed or wanted someone to be a part of my life, to be in my life, no matter what, maybe it was best that I go it alone. The loner: little ol' moi. The drift-girl. The old maid, sure. I didn't care. All I knew was that I had to get the hell away, far away. And look at me! There I was, driving and driving! I was taking the highway east. I was heading away from the city and into the mountains, the desert, I guess I was going to try and find myself. I was driving, and suddenly there were all these swirly lights around the car. Eeeks! Oh my, oh my! I woke up and I was—inside a UFO."

Tasha and I look at each other.

"We're here," Sheila says, and she brushes a hand across my leg, my upper thigh really, very delicately, the nails glancing across. She looks at me out of the corner of her eye just as Tasha looks over at Amelia, Amelia who is looking out the window and saying, "There are a lot of UFOs out there."

CHAPTER 15 . . .

"It's loud," Amelia says.

It's not exactly a bar that Sheila takes us to. It's a club, rather large but not crowded. Loud music. Well, we're here, and the seven of us take to a table. Sheila moves her body, erotically, to the music, but Amelia jounces, she's somewhere else. Tasha looks uncomfortable; she's never been one for clubs and loud music. From our table, we can look down on the dance floor, look up onto the dance level above us. There are some people gyrating away. A waiter comes by, in a tuxedo no less, and takes our order—most of us have mixed drinks, except Lisa, who sticks with wine.

The drinks come and we drink and try to talk, but it's hard over the music: we have to repeat our words and shout.

"Hey, Leonard," Amelia says.

"Yeah?"

"Wanna dance with me?" she asks.

"Sure."

So I'm dancing with her, and yes, I'm a little drunk, but that helps the matter all the more. There are bodies around us and I can fell their heat. I wish I could tune into Amelia, disregard the other dancers and pick up on her heat, her mind, her past, and her UFOs. There's something about her I can't place, something odd and distant, and yet when I look at her, her eyes closed, arms up, her body moving almost spasmodically, a if ritually, to the sounds pounding, about us, she seems like any other woman out to have a few drinks and a good time, not the person I heard tell the story of two men and the despair of disconnection. I wonder if strangers in this club look at us and think we are a couple, if they try to make quick judgments on our past and future and muse: Oh, there's a couple. I'm misguided, however, as we all know that strangers, as we ourselves are strangers to others, never give most people much thought.

I'm lost. At some point we go back to the table and I finish my drink. Tasha and I have a brief exchange—her small eyes under that dark hair—and then I'm back on the dance floor, this time with Sheila, and I'm surprised because I don't know how I got here, but there I am, again.

We're dancing closer, Sheila and I, compared to the dance I had with Amelia. Sheila is taller than Amelia, and fuller about the body, and she emits a different air, a sexual air, and the undeniable smell of attraction; or, at least, a perfume that turns me on. I start to wish I hadn't had so much to drink. In the switch from a fast to a slow song by the club's DJ, I excuse myself to go to the bathroom.

I don't realize, at first, that Sheila has followed me in.

The men's room is empty except for a guy at a urinal. There's a tap on my shoulder, I turn, almost scared, for who'd tap me here?—and see Sheila. She puts a hand on my chest, hard, pushes me toward a stall, impels me in, joins me, closes the door, locks it. She smiles.

"What are you doing?" I ask.

"Don't be dumb," she says, reaching into the pocket of her blazer.

"We're in the men's room," I say softly.

"You can't be that goofy," she says.

I'm not. I've seen women in men's rooms plenty of times, but when I was younger, at concerts, and clubs, when women would come in with a man, go to the stall to do coke and other things— And how stupid I am, yes, as I see Sheila bring out a vial of cocaine from her pocket: small, perfect, something I've seen before, like the night between Tasha, Veronica, and I.

"Want some?" she asks.

I don't know what to say. What do you say to an attractive woman face to face with you in a toilet stall, smelling pretty and sexy, and offering you drugs, touching your leg. . . .

"I stopped doing that stuff many years ago," I say.

"I'm no addict," she says, "I just like a toot now and then. Is there anything wrong with that, Leeeeeeonard?"

"No."

"You wouldn't hate me if I did some then?" she asks.

"No," I say.

She does two short blasts, one in each nostril, and when I see that look on her face, it's the past all over again, and I have the desire for some myself. I do a blast, just a short, small one, that's all, and I feel bad at first—What the hell am I doing?—but the feeling and numbness get to me and Sheila and I look at each other and we realize where we are and what we're doing and there's no denying it, there's no getting around it, we know what's going to happen next, and it does. Frantically, like creatures out of control, we kiss, tongues like two gladiators in battle. Our hands all over—hers under my shirt, me reaching into her skirt. There's no time to play with here.

"I want you," she murmurs, her warm breath to my face. I pull at her panties under her bunched-up skirt, feel her round and fleshy ass. I fall back on the toilet stall as Sheila takes my cock out. My hand briefly brushes across her sex and I feel its heat and wetness and from the light smell that reaches my nostrils I know she is more than ready. She sits on me, slides me into her, her red hair falling over my face. I realize I could be with anyone, that I am with a woman I don't even know, and we're having unsafe sex, and neither of us care, but I close my eyes, I block out the smell of the men's room and the sound of music in the club, and she could be any of the lovers I have had in my past. She could be Tasha, she could be Veronica.

I remember the look on Tasha's face as she watched me make love to Veronica. It was not a look of lust, or shock, but numb indifference, as if what she was seeing wasn't really there. She was lying on the bed next to us, and when I was done, Veronica was not; she wanted Tasha, so she kissed her, and Tasha just lay back on the bed, the same stoned look in her eyes, as Veronica made love to her with her mouth.

I remember the excitement of it, the pleasure at seeing the popular male fantasy come true, of being in bed with two women, and how I ignored the fact that while Tasha seemed to like the idea at first, that when it really began to happen she became distant, yet did not say anything to stop it from going further. Thinking of this makes me fuck Sheila harder, thrusting up as she thrusts down, so that our flesh smacks together loudly, my hands digging into her hips. I am filled with both lust and anger; the lust of memory and the moment, the anger of mistakes and the stupidity, including the stupidity of fucking my ex-wife's friend in a public toilet. It doesn't matter now.

I open her blazer, hands across her silk blouse, feel the lace bra underneath. I begin to unbutton her blouse, but instead move my hands to her ass, feeling the meat there, as we continue to fuck, energetically, drunkenly, slightly coked-up. How sleazy, I think, how perfect, for my life couldn't be anything otherwise. I remember what Tasha said to me after that night: "How would you feel if you watched another man fuck me? Or more than one man?" And I remember what I did feel: jealousy, rage, wondering if she would go out and have sex with someone just to "get back" at me—as she did, eventually, with Slater.

Sheila is coming; she puts a hand to her mouth but that doesn't muffle the sound too well, and I start to fuck her harder, and soon I reach my own orgasm, and we slow down, catch our breaths. She moves away from me, almost timidly, brushing the red hair from her face. She pulls her panties up first, then buttons her blouse and blazer, and straightens her skirt. I zip up my pants and stand. "Well," she says softly, kissing me lightly on the lips. "We better get out of here. Discreetly, if possible."

It won't be possible. We leave the stall trying to look nonchalant, which is dumb. There are three men at urinals, and one in the stall next to where we were, and another coming in just as we go out. We quickly leave the men's room and return to the lights and music.

CHAPTER 16 . . .

"Hey," Amelia says with a smile.

I don't think they notice the truth.

Sheila and I return to the table. Lisa is gone, to the bathroom we're told. I want to laugh, wondering if she went in there with some man; I try to picture this. As far as the others seem to know, Sheila and I were out on the floor all this time. I see that the number of people in here has increased. In retrospect, my liaison with Sheila was quite brief. Memory and alcohol, and other things, can fool you.

Sheila and I are good at pretending there is nothing between us but a dance. A dance, yes.

"This place is too noisy," Tasha says. She leans close to me to say this. I flinch, afraid she might smell the sex on me—I can still smell it. But what do I care? We're not married anymore, we'll never get back together. It is at this moment that I know I still love her. This makes me sad—something I'd rather not feel. I finish my drink. Tasha adds, "We were thinking of leaving, what do you think?"

"This is girls' night out," I note. "Do I have any say?"

"Well, you seem to be part of the entourage now."

"It doesn't matter to me."

Lisa returns and we discuss it. We decide to leave the club.

"Why don't we go to my place," Holly suggests.

"I've never been there," Amelia says.

"It's big and roomy and quiet," Holly says. "Also, my bar doesn't charge high prices."

"Speaking of high prices," Cara says, "I'm running low on cash—how much is a cab to your place?"

"Not a lot," Holly says, "but we can all try to cram into a

single cab. What do you think?"

"All of us," Lisa says, "into one? I don't think so."

"I've done it before," Amelia says. "It takes coordination."

"And you have to find one of those older, larger cabs," Sheila says.

"Well, heck, it sounds like fun," Cara says.

I see my ex-wife make a face.

"It's always worth a try," I tell her.

CHAPTER 17 . . .

"This is fun," says Amelia.

Somehow, we manage it. Cara and Lisa are in front with the driver; Tasha, Sheila, Amelia, Holly and I are squished into the back. It isn't so bad. I like the concentrated smell of their bodies, perfume, and what they've been drinking.

"I didn't finish my story," Amelia says.

"What story was that?" Cara asks from the front.

"When I was with Tasha and Sheila and Leonard," Amelia says. "I was telling them how I met my alien lover."

"A foreigner?" Holly says.

"No," Amelia says, "an alien from another planet. I know you probably don't believe me, but this is all so very true. Look, where was I before we got to the club?" She looks at me. I shrug.

"Er," Sheila says, "you said you were driving and then you woke up and you were inside a UFO."

"Well, I was," Amelia nods. "It was big and kind of plain and had round windows. And then The Astronaut came up to me and said, 'Hi.'"

Sheila rolls her eyes.

"I wasn't scared! I was . . . intrigued. I thought it was some wild dream or something. The Astronaut told me not to be afraid and I told him I wasn't and asked him where I was and he said, 'You're on my ship.'"

"What was his name?" Holly asks.

"The Astronaut," Amelia says, "just that, that's what he called himself, he said, 'Hello, I am The Astronaut,' and then he took off his helmet. I didn't know what to expect! I figured he would probably have two heads or weird skin or look like a fish or something, but lo! to my surprise what did I see? He was handsome! He looked just like a human, and he was this man with dark hair and—and you know what's weird, Leonard? He kind of looked like you."

"Well," I say.

"Not exactly like you, but something like you. Anyway, that's not the whole of the story, that's just the preamble. I have to get to the important stuff, like when I had sex with him."

"Sex," Sheila says. She gives me a quick glance that I think Tasha catches.

"Yes. Not at first, not just like that. You see—it was all real hazy, like some crazy dream. I dunno. I felt—seduced. He said, 'I want to show you something,' and he took my hand and we went to one of those round windows and we were looking down at the Earth, and I could see the moon, and I could see the stars, and I thought, Oh, wow, is this all real?

He said to me, 'Yes, it is very real, Amelia,' and I said, 'Hey, you can read my thoughts,' and he said, 'Yes, I can.' He said, 'I have come here just for you, Amelia, because you are the one, you have been chosen.' 'Chosen for what?' I asked. 'Chosen,' he said, and it all seemed so right. He showed me the solar system. It was awesome, to tell you the truth. We were going pretty fast, at the speed of light, I guess, because we passed by Mars and then Jupiter and then Saturn with all its rings and moons and I could see those planets so close from that window, like I could touch them, you know." She laughs. "It was like a high."

"I bet it was," Sheila says.

"Amelia—" Lisa says.

"Yeah?" from Amelia.

"Nothing."

Silence.

"He seduced me," Amelia continues softly, "and I didn't mind. I wanted it, and I knew it was going to happen. It was—what's the word? Dammit, I can't think of the word . . . Inevitable! The Astronaut said to me, 'What is about

to happen is happening because destiny dictates it as such.'
That's verbatim. Then we made love for hours—just as I had
made love with David—and it was really nice. The next thing
I knew I came to in my car and I touched my stomach and I
knew right then and there."

"Knew what?" Cara asks.

"That I was pregnant."

CHAPTER 18 . . .

Amelia says, "I always have these strange dreams that I'm getting stuck in an elevator. I think I might be claustrophobic but I'm not sure."

We're in the building Holly lives in, an uptown skyscraper, crammed in the elevator and going up.

"I was stuck in an elevator once," Cara says. "But only for twenty minutes or so."

"Alone?" Holly says.

"No, there were some other people with me."

"Any good-looking men?" Sheila asks. "If you're going to get stuck in an elevator, you better be with some good-looking men. Like several. Now wouldn't that be nice?"

Cara says, "Actually, there were two men and two women, and both the men were fat and sweaty and didn't even act like men when the elevator got stuck. They got nervous and whiny. No balls at all. It was a sorry sight."

"Well," Sheila says, "nothing ever works out the way you want it to."

The doors open.

Holly closes the door. I hear the sound echo.

She does have a very large place. I'm impressed. I wonder if she pays for this from her salary or has any family money. Looking at her, I'd say family. I won't ask. I'm always trying to assess people quickly—it's part of my job. At least I like to think it's part of my job; I'd like to think I am the kind of private eye you find in movies and books. Things would be a lot simpler that way.

Holly turns on the lights. Plush white carpet, minimal

furniture, paintings on the wall with a punk feel to them, maybe European—hell, I don't know shit about art.

There's a bar, which Holly points to, and says, "Make anything you want. But I don't have any beer."

Amelia wants to play bartendress. In fact, she says, "I worked as a waitress in a bar a long time ago." This was, of course, before she got knocked up by a spaceman.

I ask Holly where the bathroom is. I figure I better go before they all have to. Holly points down the hall, tells me to take the second left.

The bathroom smells nice. On the wall, near the shower, is a small picture of Holly with a man. A man with light black skin. Holly looks younger, hair shorter, and they are both smiling at the camera, holding one another. I wonder what happened; they both look so happy in this moment. But that's all it really comes down to, I think: moments. We live lives of moments, not the neat construct of uniformity that, say, the silver screen gives us. Maybe Holly will tell us her story with this man.

I unzip my pants and begin to pee into the toilet, trying not to think of anything, but I can feel the dried product of Sheila's sex on my cock, and I can faintly smell it, and this makes me start to think. I think again about Veronica, who was Tasha's friend at first, and later became my friend. Hell, she was my lover—that one night. But no, no, no—funny how memory plays tricks with you. There was another time, when Veronica and I had gotten together to discuss what happened, maybe try to make some sense out of it, and we made love, alone, together, away from the watching eyes of my wife. This happened before Tasha had told me what she'd done with Frederick Slater.

I hear a scream. Holly's scream, I believe, a short burst, like one of surprise—and then several other small screams. Then silence.

I zip up and listen. I hear muffled words, can't make anything out.

I open the bathroom door, slowly, quietly, instinct and

experience telling me not to be quick or loud. I hear a man's voice saying something. I move down the hall, see the six women by the bar, and the back of a man wearing a raincoat and large black shoes. He's holding a knife. He has graying hair.

"How the hell did you get into my apartment?" Holly says, trying to sound tough but not doing a good job of it.

"I can do a lot of things," the man says. "I'm a talented guy."

His voice is deep but uncertain. He's probably just as scared as they are. He was expecting her to come home alone, had no idea she'd have so much company.

I move slowly.

"You're crazy," Holly says. "You're getting yourself into deep shit."

"What does it matter?" he says, waving the knife. "I just lost my fucking job because of you. I won't ever get another job like it in the field. Because of you, you fucking cunt-bitch."

"You caused the trouble yourself," Holly says. "You got caught."

"And you expected me to just take it like it's nothing?"

"Buddy," Sheila says, "you need professional help."

"Fuck you!"

"Put that knife away, please," Holly says.

The man says, "Oh? Does it scare you, bitch?"

"There are six of us here," Holly says. "What do you plan to do? Kill us all?"

"Maybe I will," he answers, but I know from his voice that he isn't going to do anything.

Amelia sees me coming up behind him. Her face registers this. I have to act fast before he catches on and turns.

I overtake him easily, too easily. I grab his arm, slap the knife from his hand before he knows what's happening. He tries to turn and swing, tries to kick. I slug him a good one in the stomach. He doubles over. I wrestle him to the ground, pin his arm behind his back until he gags and wheezes and pleads for me to let him go.

"You're hurting me!" he whimpers.

"Yay!" Amelia claps her hands and jumps up and down, like a cheerleader.

Both Lisa and Tasha lean against the bar, the color coming back to their skin.

"Call the police," I say.

"I'm doing it," Holly says, picking up the phone.

"Let go of me," the man protests. Whine, whine.

"Who is this guy?" I ask.

"The creep who was sending me the harassing e-mail," Holly says.

CHAPTER 19 . . .

"It's like a movie," is Amelia's commentary.

The police come and reports are filed; we're all asked questions and we give them our accounts of the story. One of the detectives on site smirks when I show him my P.I. license. "Always good to play hero in front of a bunch of lasses, eh?" He winks at me.

The man, who'd been stalking Holly over a computer and now in real life, is taken away. Holly assures us that she will be pressing charges profusely. "I want that asshole put away," she says.

"He'll be doing some time," another detective tells her. "Breaking and entering, intent of assault and harm, compounded with the sexual harassment charges from your job. He's going down."

Right. He'll cut a deal. They always do. This is a busy city with very crowded courts.

The whole process takes a little more than an hour. The seven of us are left alone. Maybe we could pretend as if none of this ever happened. I could. The mood of the group isn't the same. We're all sobered up now, that's for sure.

"Leonard," Holly says, "am I glad you were here. All of you. I don't even want to think about what would've happened to me if I'd been alone."

"Don't think about it at all," Lisa tells her. "If you dwell on what might've happened, you'll go nuts."

"It's hard not to," Holly says.

Sheila looks at me and says, "The man of the hour."

I wave a hand. "Can I get a drink?"

"Whatever you want," Holly says, and she's at the bar.

"Tequila tonic," I say.

"Me, too," from Amelia.

"Whatever you want," Sheila says. I don't know what she's getting at.

"I don't understand how that sonofabitch got into my place!" Holly says.

"He's a hacker—a good one," I say. "He got past the doorman—not always a hard thing to do. You have a keycard slot—he knows electronics. How he got in is no mystery, and he'll probably tell the cops. He'll want to brag."

"You come across a lot of this in your profession?" Lisa asks me, the writer at work.

"Actually," I say, "no."

"In any event," Holly says, "I'm glad you were here. I'm grateful, really." She hands me a drink.

"I'll bill you," I say seriously.

She looks at me.

Smile. "Kidding."

There's a tense silence, the tension from elsewhere. Then they all laugh—hollowly.

CHAPTER 20 . . .

The night is ruined. Lisa and Cara call a cab and leave. Plans are made to meet next Thursday, same place and time. I don't think I'll be there. I don't belong there, and I don't belong here.

But I need another drink before I get on my way, and so do Tasha and Sheila.

"Will you be okay?" Tasha asks Holly.

"Yes, thank you," Holly says.

"I'll stay here tonight if you want me to," Tasha says.

"He's behind bars," Holly says. "I think I'm safe tonight."

Amelia and I look at each other. She smiles, almost shyly, and looks away.

"I'll call us a cab," Sheila says, picking up the phone.
*****

I'm in the front seat with the driver. I feel odd, and the driver gives me a look, and then glances at the three women in the back of the cab.

"I still can't believe that really happened," from Amelia.

"The world," Sheila sighs. "People can really be fucked up at times."

Amelia says, "We were lucky Leonard was there."

"Yes," Sheila joins in, "weren't we?" There's no mistaking the edge in her voice.

The driver wants to know who's going home first and where, or are we going to the same place? I turn to the three women, realizing that we are all still pretty much riding on adrenaline and not sure what we're doing, where we're going. But it's late and home is the place to go when it's late.

"I guess I live the closest," Sheila says with a shrug,

*   *   *

"The funny thing about being pregnant by an alien," Amelia says, "is that it didn't feel any different. I guess that's a silly thing to say since I'd never actually been pregnant before, so I can't really make a comparison. What I mean is that it didn't feel like I was pregnant by something from another world. Maybe I don't know what I'm talking about. How can I best describe it? It felt natural, that's all. It felt like the most natural thing—and I was happy, believe it or not. I was happy even if my alien lover had left me on earth and gone back to the stars, left me with a baby growing inside. I kept wondering if the gestation period might be quicker, like a couple of months, but it was nine months, just like a normal pregnancy.

"But how did Nick react to all this? Well, after the encounter with David, it's pretty obvious, you know, that the relationship—if you can really call it a relationship—was kaput. But especially now, since I had been abducted by The Astronaut that very same night, made love to him and conceived. It was the end of one thing and the beginning of another. It was like I was another person now, a new person, a person with no history or past. I knew my name was no longer Amelia; it had been changed to Amnesia."

Silence in the cab, an odd silence. I wonder what the driver thinks of Amelia's monologue, if it's unusual for him to hear something like it. Then again, he's a cab driver. For him, we're all just another group of people in the city moving from cab to cab like Bedouins in the desert of what we think is the human heart.

I feel as if Amelia is waiting for someone to prompt her to continue. I'm not sure if I want her to. I don't think I care. Her voice is rather soothing, a distraction from my own thoughts and memories. I'm thinking of Veronica.

Veronica should be here with us.

Maybe Veronica is somewhere with aliens.

"While I was pregnant," Amelia says, "I wound up living with David and his wife for a while. His wife Eileen. Can you believe that? I know it sounds weird. It was weird, but I did it. It was almost like I became a part of their family."

"So," Tasha says, brushing the hair out of her eyes, "how did this come about? His wife had to know there was something going on between the two of you."

"She knew," Amelia says, nodding. "In fact, she'd always known. I wasn't the only extramarital affair David had. There had been others, and even I knew this. David was a great guy—I still love him—but he was incapable of being faithful."

Perhaps like Slater, I think.

"He was a pussy hound," Sheila says.

"Maybe, but it wasn't that superficial. Eileen knew about it and tolerated it, I suppose, because she loved him so much. Maybe like Lisa's mother—she knew of the infidelities, but knew the affairs were only for the moment. David loved Eileen, and however things went, he always went back to her. He went back home because home was safe and warm.

"But now I was in their home. I had showed up at their door. It was like I was outside myself, like I was watching myself. Because I didn't know who I was. I said to them, when they answered the door, 'Who am I and why am I here?' I was drawn to their home, like it was a magnet, like I could go there to find the answers I was searching for.

"I really can't say what happened from there," she adds. "I know Eileen wasn't happy about it."

CHAPTER 21 . . .

"But I wound up living with them," Amelia says. "For a while anyway."

The cab stops before a brownstone building; this is Sheila's stop. She begins to open her purse and get money, but I wave at her and tell her I'll pay for the cab. She looks uncertain, then nods, an inaudible "thanks" on her lips.

"Well, guys," Sheila says, "it's been fun."

"Take care," from Amelia.

"You too, hon. Later," she adds, to Tasha, and Tasha nods. As Sheila gets out, she slyly slips me a business card. I watch her as she goes up the stairs, takes out a set of keys, and goes in. The cab begins to move to our next destination.

"I wish I was more like Sheila," Amelia says. "She seems to have control of her life. She figures out what she wants and then goes out and takes it."

I think about the deception of appearances; I want to say something about it, but I have neither the inclination nor the words.

"I've never really had control over anything," Amelia says. "Seems like all my life others have been calling the shots. They've had more control over my destination than I'd rather admit. Like The Astronaut, for example. I had no intentions either of sleeping with him or carrying his baby, but he had it all planned. He said it was destiny, but it was really about power.

"When I was living with David and Eileen, I began to understand the strange motions of power. I wasn't myself, I was Amnesia, and I didn't know anything other than that I was living with a married couple and my belly was getting bigger. At first Eileen was completely against having me in their home. That was understandable, of course. But David told her, 'We can't turn her out to the world now that she doesn't know who she is.' Eileen was a really sweet, and weak, person, and she gave in, and I was put in the guest room and, as the months went on, my stomach got big with the alien's child.

"In the end, Eileen and I became close. Very close. We could have been lovers—there was that tension. David now became upset because he felt distant from this friendship. The balance of power had tipped the other way; his meek wife and former lover were no longer strangers but allies.

"But I soon began to remember who I was. I wasn't Amnesia after all, I was Amelia. Me. And I was knocked up and I remembered by whom and when one night David yelled at me, yelled at us both really, I decided I had to leave. I had to go. I had to be somewhere alone to have my baby.

"I remembered I had a little money left in the bank so I went to get it and left my new family and went solo to be a family all by myself, with the alien baby in my belly. I thought I could hide. But I knew I couldn't hide from him. He found me."

"Who?" Tasha says. "David?"

"No. The Astronaut. He came back for me, when I was ready to give birth. He took me back into his spaceship and there were doctors of his kind there. I had the baby—a girl—and The Astronaut took her from me. I couldn't believe he was doing this! But he said it was for the best; the child would have special powers and would be very different from other children on this planet, and needed to grow up with her kind. I asked him to take me with him, with them—I didn't want to be separated from my child, and maybe I was still in love with this spaceman. But The Astronaut told me this wasn't possible. He said I had to go back to Earth and life my life. 'How can I live my life,' I asked, 'when you're taking a part of it away?' 'You will,' he said. So I was put back in this world and tried my best to get on with the rest of my life. I told myself no more married men, no more meaningless sex. I went back to school and got my teaching degree and here I am now, trying to live the best way I can."

Amelia looks out the window and at the sky, and says, "I wonder what she's doing up there, my daughter. I wonder what life is like for her on that faraway planet. I wonder if she's ever heard the loud ticking of a clock: tick-tock-tock tick-tock goes the clock."

CHAPTER 22 . . .

"See ya," Amelia says as she leaves the cab and goes into the building she lives.

"I'm just two blocks away," Tasha says to the driver, and gives him her address. I turn to look at her. One eye is covered with hair; her other eye glances at me in the darkness of the car. I think I should move into the back with her. It feels right at the moment, but the cab goes—and then it's too late. It's a short ride to her home.

"Have you talked to Veronica lately?" Tasha asks.

"No," I say.

"Really?"

"Things change," I say. "The balance of power, like your friend said. Sometimes things don't work out the way you'd like, like your other friend said. You have wise friends these days." I feel stupid.

"Yes," Tasha says, "I know."

Silence.

"When you see or talk to her again," she says, "tell her I said hi."

"I will."

"Tell her—tell her I hope things are okay."

"Things will never ultimately be okay for her."

"And you?" she asks.

I don't know what to say, except "Tasha—" I turn to look at her.

"Yes?" she asks.

The cab stops.

*****

I want to walk her to her door, but she tells me no, she'll

be okay. She won't look at me. My ex-wife doesn't even say good night, only, "We'll talk." Then she's gone.

"A looker," the cabby says.

I give him my address.

He drives. He could drive forever and I wouldn't care.

"You folks are the nicest I've had in the car all night," the cabby tells me. "I've had some wild ones tonight. Dunno what it is. Maybe a full moon? I don't see none. I guess it's just one of those nights."

"Yeah," I say.

CHAPTER 23 . . .

I get my mail and look through it, hoping for a surprise, something to intrigue me; it's the same crap as always. I go to the fridge, get a beer; when I open it, I think of Amelia. It would be nice, perhaps, to have Amelia here and share a beer with her; she could tell me more of her weird stories.

I need stories. We all need stories. I don't feel good facing the silence, the lack of human interaction, in the retirement of my small apartment.

There are a couple of messages on the answering machine. One is from someone I haven't talked to in a while. I wonder why she's calling. I don't think I want to call her back. The rest of the messages have to do with possible jobs. I drink my beer and look out the window, seeing a part of the city. It's such a fucking big place; I've never really given it a great deal of thought.

I haven't given a lot of things much thought, until tonight.

I find Sheila's card in my pocket. Office number printed, home number handwritten. I can still smell her on me.

I almost stop myself. But I call her.

"Were you asleep?" I ask.

"No," she says. "I was hoping you'd call. I knew you would."

"I almost didn't."

"You're teasing me."

"I feel strange," I say.

"Why?" Then, "Don't get the wrong idea. About what happened tonight. That's not something I do often. Really, that's like the second time I've ever done anything so sponta-neous and—dangerous. What can I say? I find you attractive, and at that moment I wanted you. I had to have you. So I took you."

"And how do you feel now?"

"We're talking, aren't we?" she says.

"We are."

"It's silly to play little games," she says. "We're adults: we know the moves and what needs to be done. Do you get what I mean?" She adds, "I'd like to see you again. If you don't want to see me, tell me."

"I'm attracted to you too," I say, "but—"

"Is it Tasha?"

I don't know.

"You're not married to her anymore," Sheila says.

"No."

"And I don't think you two get along all that well."

"Maybe that's it."

"Tasha's a big girl. She can handle it. And does anyone have to know?"

"They'll find out."

"Do you think I'd tell?"

"Would you?"

She laughs softly, "Well, I just might."

Pause.

"So," she says.

"So," I say.

She says, "Here we are."

Pause.

"Leonard," she asks, "do you want to know something?"

"What?"

"I'm lying on my bed right now," she says, "and I'm naked under my robe. I'm touching myself."

CHAPTER 24 . . .

"I'm touching myself," she says, "but I'm thinking of you, thinking of your hands touching me. Thinking about this gets me hot."

"Where are you touching yourself?"

Her voice lowers. "Where do you think, you fool?"

"I can think of several places."

"My robe is partially opened," she says. "My legs are open. I'm touching my legs, my upper legs, my thighs. And I'm slowly getting to the gold, the good stuff. You know the good stuff, baby; you had some tonight."

I can smell it.

"But this could be you touching me," she says. "This should be you touching me, right here, right now, tonight, this night, this hot night. Your hands or tongue, moving up, making me happy, making me go into a frenzy." She breathes heavily. "It feels good," she says.

"I know," I say.

"Lightly, I'm touching my pussy," she says. "I'm touching the lips of my pussy and already I'm wet and wanting you."

"Tell me more."

"What do you want to know? I'll tell you anything."

"Tell me anything," I say. "Tell me everything."

"I'm thinking of putting a finger in my pussy."

"Then why don't you?"

"I will if you want me to."

I say, "I want you to."

She says, "Why don't you take my hand, take it and put it there, make me put my finger in."

"I would if I was there."

She says, "You are here."

"I'm grabbing your hand and pressing it to your cunt," I say, "and making you put a finger, a long finger, deep into your cunt."

A sigh and then, "It's in, my finger's in."

"Move it in and out."

"I'm doing it . . . and it feels so good." She says, "Kiss me, Leonard."

"I kiss you," I say. "I am kissing you."

"Our tongues touch."

"You want to put two fingers in your cunt; you're thinking about it."

"I want to, yes."

"Do it."

"Help me."

"I am, can't you feel it?"

"Yes," she hisses. "I have two fingers in my pussy and it feels so, so good."

I say, "I'd like to put my mouth down there, taste you as you touch yourself."

"Then do it," she says. "Do you think I'd stop you? You can do whatever you want. I won't stop you. I'm giving myself up to you."

"Would you let me hurt you if I wanted to?"

"Do you want to hurt me?"

Pause.

"My mouth is at your cunt," I tell her, "and I lick, lightly, and I'm tasting your cunt and your fingers."

"I put one of my fingers into your mouth."

"I like that."

"Suck on it."

"I am; I'm sucking on that finger like I want to suck on your clit."

"Are you hard?" she asks.

Pause.

"Yes."

"You're hard and I'm wet," she says, "and we're both

turned on and what will we do about this, lover?"

"I'm going to your clit," I say to her, "and I'm sucking on it."

"Not too hard."

"No."

"I like that."

"I want you to come."

"Oh, I'll come," she says softly, "but I want you to do the same. Maybe come with me, baby. Your dick is hard. Do you have it out? Are you playing with it like I'm playing with myself?"

"Take it out," I say. "Take it out and put it in your mouth."

"Do you want me on my knees?"

"I want you any way possible."

"I take your hard cock and hold it in my hand. With my other hand, I rub your balls."

"I move the tip of it to your lips."

"I open my mouth and take it," she says, "I suck on your hard prick. It's hot in my mouth."

"Yes," I say.

"Are you going to come in my mouth?"

"Do you want me to?"

"I want to taste you," she says. "I want you inside me, all over and inside me. I want you to come everywhere, come all night. We can both come all night, because we have all night. When we're together, things are nice; together we're shielded and safe."

CHAPTER 25 . . .

I lie in my bed, thinking I shouldn't be here. My body is clean; I just had a shower. I close my eyes and can't sleep. I hear Sheila's voice in my head, then Veronica's; I want them both to go away.

The phone rings. I reach for it.

"Hello."

"I had to call."

"I know."

"You knew I was going to call."

"Sooner or later," I tell my ex-wife, "I knew you would. It was in the air tonight."

"Maybe I shouldn't be calling."

"I was just thinking of you."

She says, "Why are you lying to me?"

"The truth. I was thinking of you, and I was thinking of a lot of other things. You know what I was really thinking about?"

"What?"

"Your little group," I say. "You six women. I was thinking how great it is that you get together like that once a week and talk about things. Even with me there, you were all so open and honest. It was refreshing. I was thinking that there should have been someone with you, there should have been a seventh woman in your group. Veronica should've been there. If she'd had such a group—"

"Yes, I know," she says.

I say, "I was thinking that Veronica would have gotten a kick out of Amelia's wild stories. Amelia doesn't really believe all that crap, does she?"

"Amelia needs some help before it gets worse," Tasha says. "Wasn't it obvious to you what she was really saying?"

"No."

"And you call yourself a private eye! She told us about that guy, David, right? Well, he's the one who got her pregnant. I don't know if she really lived with David and his wife, maybe she did, but she's never been able to face the truth about it. She was pregnant by a married man and the child was a stillbirth."

"Jesus."

"So instead of dealing with the matter realistically, she makes up some crazy story about an alien and a spaceship and that her baby is really on some other planet. So she doesn't have to feel the pain," Tasha says. "Besides, it's easier to talk about. Bullshit makes us cowards."

"I see what you mean," I say.

"She does need to see someone who can help her. The girls and I were going to bring this up to her soon. We were going to bring it up tonight, but you were there so maybe it'll be next week—"

"I'd like to go next week—"

"No," she says.

"—but I shouldn't. I don't belong."

"You were a fluke. You had to be in the same bar, didn't you?"

"Just a fluke."

"I might suggest we not go to the same bar next week."

"I get the hint," I say.

"Sorry. I didn't mean to be harsh."

"It's not like I'm going to follow you or anything."

"I didn't call to fight," she says.

"Why did you call?"

"I'm not sure."

"You don't want to say."

"I don't know how to say."

"Just say it."

"I don't have any words."

"You work in publishing. You have all the words in the world, all the words anyone would ever want or need."

"Maybe," she says. "Listen—"

CHAPTER 26 . . .

I know it before she says it. "I was also thinking that Veronica might've fit in well with our group," Tasha says, "and I was—I was wondering if you'd heard from her lately. I know I asked, but tell me the truth, Leonard, really."

"Why would I have heard from her?"

"I—" she begins.

"Have you?" I ask.

"Would I be asking you if—"

"Tell me the truth. Tell me what you're thinking." I hate it when people are elusive.

"Sometimes," she says, "I used to think the two of you got together behind my back and were lovers."

"We did once," I say, "but that was after you left me, and it was only once, and it felt like a bad mistake. It was a bad mistake. I don't think either of us knew what we were doing exactly. The motions of silly shadows. But I told you this before, remember?"

"It was just once?"

"Why would I lie?" I say. "Especially now?"

"Sorry," she says. "I should trust you. I always trusted you. I think. Even if I didn't act like I did, I did. You never used to lie to me, did you? Like I lied to you. I didn't really lie to you. I just told you the truth when it was too late. I should have told you the truth when things happened, but I was scared."

"Frederick Slater," I say.

"It was horrible seeing him tonight. It was a nightmare. I didn't know what I'd do if—"

"He didn't see us."

"Are you sure?"

"Does it matter?"

"I guess not."

"You haven't been seeing him?" I ask.

"I see him around," she says, "but I haven't been sleeping with him if that's what you mean."

"Are you sleeping with anyone now?"

Pause.

Probably a bad question.

She says, "I ended a relationship two months ago. It wasn't much of a relationship, though. What about you?" she asks cautiously.

"Nothing worth talking about," I say.

"Will you start something with Sheila?" she asks.

There's that kind of silence you just loathe.

"I'm not stupid or blind," Tasha says, "I could see what was going on between you two. The looks. It started from the beginning, when you first sat down. Sheila is a man-chaser; she always has been. I could tell you some stories about her, but I won't. Maybe she'll tell you them herself. You can't deny this was happening, and I'm sure I wasn't the only one to notice. The two of you disappeared from the dance floor."

"There's nothing between us," I say. This is no lie. I know it now. Despite what has gone on with Sheila and myself both in person and on the phone, I have no desire to have further contact with her. I would rather touch my ex-wife.

"There could be," she says, "if you want it."

"Maybe I don't want it."

"She's pretty, and energetic."

"Do you think that's what I want?"

"What," Tasha says, "do you want?"

She asked me the same question that night with Veronica. We were drunk and high and on the bed; I don't know how it started, but it did. I think it began as a joke, maybe I started it, said something like, "Why don't we have a threesome?" and the next thing I knew we were in bed, kissing and pulling at each other's clothes. "What do you want?" Tasha asked; I only knew, that moment, that I wanted them both. "I want you," Veronica told Tasha and Tasha became numb. I can still see the look on my ex-wife's face, see it now as I hear her voice.

"I want a lot of things," I say.

"I want a few things that I've lost," Tasha says. "I'm happy with my life, but there are things missing. Things that used to be there. I want them back."

CHAPTER 27 . . .

"Seeing you tonight," she says, "made me think of those things. I haven't been able to sleep. I feel strange. Sad. I know this is probably the wrong thing to say, Leonard, but I miss you—sometimes."

I say, "I do, too."

"Please don't misunderstand me."

"I'm not."

"You don't even know what I'm talking about."

"Yes, I do."

"No," she says, "you don't."

"Are we arguing?" I ask.

"No," she says, "I don't think so."

"We used to have some good arguments."

"Yes," she says. "Constructive ones, no violence or anger, just a good butting of the heads."

"Those were good buttings."

"That's something I miss," she says, "but I also miss our friendship. We were lovers, we were married, but we were also friends. Weren't we? I seem to remember it that way."

"Yes," I say, "we were."

"Why did things have to change? Why did that have to happen with Veronica?"

"It just happened," I say.

"I don't feel as distant from it as I'd like to," Tasha says. "I can still feel . . . all those mixed feelings, and they scare me. But I miss her, too. I miss Veronica because she was a friend, a good friend, and she was always there, she cared for us and we cared for her and—"

"And maybe that's why it happened," I say.

"Sometimes I think I overreacted," she says, "but also, I don't think I did. I was being me. I should've stopped it—stopped us—as it happened, I should've done something, but I let it go on and I felt so dirty afterwards, and I couldn't look at you the same, I couldn't feel for you the same, I couldn't do it anymore."

"And you slept with Slater," I say.

"Once."

"Once," I say.

"Like you slept with Veronica again."

"And then she went away," I say, "like they all go away."

"I miss her," she says.

"I know."

"And I," Tasha says, "miss you, too."

I listen to her breath.

"What are you doing?" I ask. "Right now?"

"I'm looking in my fridge. Do you know what I have? I have some vodka Jell-o."

"You still make that?" I remember the taste of it.

"I still make it. I have a lot of it here."

"Well," I say, "sounds like a good time to snack."

She says, "But how much vodka Jell-O can a girl eat?"

I laugh.

"You bastard," she says. "Why did you have to be with us there tonight? Do you think I need this?"

"I'm sorry."

"Don't be sorry! You always say that! There's nothing to be sorry about! But you're still a bastard!"

"Yes," I say. "I am."

"You don't need to agree with me."

"I'd like to hold you right now," I tell her. "You're crying and I'd like to hold you so you could cry on me."

"That sounds nice," she says.

"It would feel right."

Breathing.

"What would you do," I ask, "if I came over there right now? If I knocked on your door? Would you answer it?"

"Of course."

"Would you let me in?"

"I might."

"Yes or no."

"I wouldn't let you stand outside in the cold," she says. "I'm not a cruel person."

"I might just come over right now," I say. "I just might."

"Don't."

"I'd regret it if I didn't."

"Leonard."

"Yes."

"Let me come over there," she says. "I'll come over there. I'll come to you. That'd be better."

"Will you?"

"I called," she says.

"Will you let me hold you?"

"I want to be held," she says. "But if I knock on your door, will you answer?"

"Yes."

"Will you let me in?"

"Yes."

"Can I cry on you?"

"You can cry with me."

She says my name and hangs up; and I look at the door to my apartment knowing she won't come over, she won't knock, and I won't let her in.

ABOUT THE AUTHOR . . .

Michael Hemmingson writes books in every possible genre he can: literary, western, SF, horror, noir, autobiography, erotica, narrative journalism, gonzo journalism, cultural anthropology, critical theory, critifiction, ethnography, and many other modes of academia including post-postmodern and post-colonial treatises. And private eye yarns. And film and TV studies. And smut. He also writes plays and screenplays. He has two independent feature films out: *The Watermelon* (LightSong Films) and *Stations* (Hemlene Entertainment). He has produced, directed, and written plays in San Diego and Los Angeles for the Fritz Theater and The Alien Stage Project. He lives in southern California, where the dead and the unborn visit him nightly as his two cats (Worf and Poe) observe with indifferent, feline curiosity.

www.ingramcontent.com/pod-product-compliance
Lightning Source LLC
Chambersburg PA
CBHW052149170626
46812CB00004B/1658